E.O.S.:

End of Sentence

E.O.S.:

End of Sentence

Adrian "Ox" Mendez

www.urbanbooks.net

Urban Books, LLC
300 Farmingdale Road, NY-Route 109
Farmingdale, NY 11735

ISBN 13: 978-1-64556-567-3

First Mass Market Printing May 2024
First Trade Paperback Printing May 2023
Printed in the United States of America

10 9 8 7 6 5 4 3 2 1

Distributed by Kensington Publishing Corp.
Submit Orders to:
Customer Service
400 Hahn Road
Westminster, MD 21157-4627
Phone: 1-800-733-3000
Fax: 1-800-659-2436

This book is dedicated to my son, Tashawn Mendez, who has proved to have the endurance and decision-making ability that most grown men lack by not being your daddy but striving to be better than your daddy.

I love you, fatboy!

A NOTE FROM THE AUTHOR

Real talk!

Statistics say that over 57 percent of individuals released from incarceration will return within nine months for committing another crime. Unfortunately, the prison system is a revolving door for those who, for whatever reason, are not found acceptable by society. Those of us who have been unfortunate enough to be imprisoned at one point in our life should use that experience as a stepping stone toward a better tomorrow by telling stories of the dark world of consequences rather than the temporary glories of being a thug. Let those who still have a choice to avoid it know that, due to careless actions, simple things like taking a shit, eating food of your choice, and the other basic rights of a human being will be taken from you. While incarcerated, I was given a jewel of wisdom from my grandmother through a letter that goes, "Going There cannot tell Been There how to Get There, so it is up to Been There to show Going

There the right way." Being that I have Been There, I can tell anyone Going There that there are much better places to go!

Never forget those who are waiting for their "end of sentence" date. When you get home, stay home and play your part so that younger "thugs" can know that they can do better.

CHAPTER ONE

"Ma, how much longer until we get there?" Junior exclaimed out of frustration. They had been sitting on the same bus for what felt like hours. "You said it wasn't gonna take much longer after this," he whined.

"We'll be there soon," Kera reassured her son. She could sense the frustration in his voice. She couldn't blame him. They had been on the road for hours. They were almost there though. She just needed Junior to be a little bit more patient and hold on a bit longer.

Kera thought about what she could say or do to buy more time. "Didn't I tell you to download long movies so you wouldn't get bored on the ride here? I told you we were going to be a while on the bus. The train ride was the first part. I warned you about the second part," she reminded her son.

No matter how many times they did this, he always had something to say. Never mind the fact that they had been doing this for almost three years in a row. Kera had to deal with the same complaints every year. The only difference was that, as time went on, Junior would get less and less patient. It seemed like with every trip they took Junior would ask more and more questions and only get more and more impatient with them getting to their destination.

Kera wasn't sure how much of this she could handle. She knew that her man had less than six months to go, but she was hanging on by a thread.

"Are you done watching the movie you downloaded?" she questioned her son.

"No, I still have about an hour left," Junior admitted. He was frustrated with the ride. He was looking forward to seeing his dad, but he was completely done with how long it took to get to him. He was starting to get frustrated with the fact that the only way to see his father was when he and his mother spent damn near half a day taking trains and buses to see him. He loved his dad and always looked forward to seeing him, but the older he got, the more frustrated he felt with trying to understand his father's life choices. He knew better than to bring any of this up to his mom though. His mom was just trying to make the best out of the hand she was dealt.

"It's cool. If anything, I'll just listen to some music until we get there," he said to his mom, realizing she must have been tired and nervous as they made their way to see his father. The last thing he wanted was to make his mother any more anxious or nervous than necessary.

"Okay, good," his mother replied.

"I'm sorry, but the number you are trying to reach is not in service at this time. Please check the number and dial again."

After four attempts of making sure the right number was being dialed and checking his PIN code each time, Pain hung up the phone and walked back to his bunk with three words on his mind: *what the fuck?* Just last week he'd dialed the same number and spoken to his sweetheart, Kera. Something didn't make sense. Kera had worked her ass off to be able to add that line. After three years of his forty-eight-month bid, she finally got herself in a position to have an extra phone line installed so it could be easier for them to stay in contact. She did all of that just so Pain could call to hear one of the few voices that brought him comfort.

"Daddy, no matter what you are going through, I will always be in your corner. I love you, baby. I am waiting for you and you only," Kera had recited as if from a script. Every time they talked, she made it a point to reassure him that she was there for him no matter what. She especially understood that with Pain's recent loss, he needed all the support that she could offer.

“I’m good. Just gotta stay focused and do what I gotta do,” Pain had replied. He heard Kera take a deep breath on the other side. He knew she hated when he shut down and didn’t talk about his emotions. “I’m all right, babe. I love you too,” he added, hoping that would help her feel a little better.

It wasn’t that he didn’t want to talk about things. It was just really hard for him to open up. Since he was 16, he had built a mental wall that made Mount Everest look like a speed bump. He’d seen and been through a lot from when he was a little boy. One thing he’d learned early on was that people couldn’t be trusted and would be quick to take advantage if he showed any type of weakness. It wasn’t that he didn’t trust Kera. She was actually one of the few people he felt like he could be himself around. It was that he didn’t know how to. He found it very hard to express himself. Even though he was as complex as a Chinese puzzle, she loved him to a point where the challenges no longer seemed like a challenge. It was more like knowing the pass code to a vault with countless locks. It took a special type of locksmith to get to his deepest hidden treasures.

“My nigga, if you ain’t gonna go, I’ll be happy to go out there to keep little mama’s company. Shit, my people ain’t coming to see me.” The voice of his roommate snapped Pain back to reality. Real was one of the few niggas on the pound Pain could vibe with. He was also a New York nigga who got caught slipping in the South. Just like Pain, Real never let where he was change where he was from. He represented Brooklyn to the fullest.

"Inmate Phillips, Javon Phillips, report to the visitation park," the nasal voice over the intercom repeated.

"You act like you in some kind of Jedi Knight trance. Come back to earth, son." Real knew his dawg was deep in thought and didn't want his boy to get stuck in his head. He knew that Pain was feeling the loss of his brother and wanted to be left alone, but at the same time he couldn't let his boy just sit in the slumps. He also knew it gave Pain comfort when his girl came to visit him.

"My bad. I was out there for a minute. I'm just fucked up right now, and shit seems to be getting worse," Pain said while walking to the sink to wash his face to bring him all the way back to reality. He did his best to avoid seeing his reflection in the mirror. Last week he put a towel over the dull mirror above the sink because the reflection was only a painful reminder of his loss.

"You know them crackas are gonna trip about that towel. Sooner or later you gonna have to face the man in the mirror," Real told him that day. Real could see Pain going through it mentally and felt like he had to keep an eye on his boy to make sure he didn't get too depressed.

"I should have been there for him. I see him every time I look in the mirror. It feels like he is looking at me, begging for help. Help that I can't give him because I'm locked in this shit hole." Pain was close to tears as he grabbed on to the sides of the sink.

"Son, I ain't know bro at all, but one thing I do know from experience is that the only thing you can do for the dead is to live life. That's real talk from a real nigga." Real always found a way to slide his catchphrase in every conversation. Sometimes it was an annoying gimmick, like the clock that Flavor Flav hung around his neck, but this time the words had some deep meaning.

Ten minutes later Pain was finally dressed in class A uniform, headed to the bubble to get his pass for the visitation park.

"You think you are fucking royalty or something?" barked the five-foot-six guard from inside of the reinforced bubble. "I have been paging you for damn near half an hour, and you come dragging your sorry ass up here now expecting me to jump for you?" Provoking the inmates was his pastime, just to see one lose their cool so he could back up their release date with bullshit paperwork.

Pain made up his mind a long time ago that these crackas weren't gonna get a single extra day from him. With a cold stare, Pain looked through the glass at the officer, trying to hold his composure and thinking, *pussy cracka, on the street you would run the other way if you saw my shadow. You got it for now, but you better pray I never catch your ass out there!*

"My bad. I was asleep and didn't hear you calling, sir." Deciding to pacify the officer, Pain gave a humble answer, knowing that he had no wins right now.

"Next time you can just stay asleep and we'll send that bitch home or, better yet, take her to my house so I can put her fat ass in the buck." Pushing the pass through the window, the guard was trying to make Pain lose his cool, but this inmate wouldn't bite the bait.

Entering the visitation park, Pain kept his head straight forward toward Kera and J.J., knowing the worst thing was for another inmate to think he was eye fucking their visitors. Insecurities about their old ladies being unfaithful on the streets was bad enough without having a nigga looking them up and down like a piece of meat.

Kera gave her man a big hug and a quick kiss. Too much affection wasn't allowed and could lead to a termination of a visit. "Hey, big daddy, I thought you wasn't coming out. What were you doing, putting on makeup?" Kera always threw humor at her man to bring out the foxlike grin that was the closest thing to a smile he would give.

"Queen of comedy, queen of comedy. Don't let me get another charge up in here for domestic violence." He quickly delivered a playful slap on her ass, which went undetected by the guards. He gave her the grin he knew she was looking for.

"What up, man? You act like you about to pull out a burner and lay the whole park down," he said to Junior while throwing phantom punches at his 13-year-old son.

"Pop, you know how I do. I'm just peeping out the area." Junior landed a two piece right into his father's chest.

"He think he is a real gangster. You need to talk to his little ass before them boys at school do something serious to him." Kera looked at Junior to let him know that she was about to let his pops know the current events.

"Slow down, mama. Little man can handle himself just as well as his old man," said Pain while counteracting the punches in the chest with three light taps with open hands to Junior's chin and the top of his head.

"That's the same attitude that had that Haitian boy's mother at my doorstep showing me his busted lip and black eye while cussing me out in Creole," Kera said with a hand on her hip, waiting for disciplinary words from Pain.

While he grinned, the next words out of Pain's mouth were, "You should have told her son to either tighten up his fight game or send the little punk to ballet school where he can prance around like the fairy he is."

Realizing it was a dead issue, Kera threw her hands in the air and let out a sigh of defeat. She should have known better than to try to make Pain straighten out Junior's behavior. Why should he? Javon Jr. not only looked like his father, but he was his father in every aspect, especially his attitude. Pain didn't take shit from anyone, and neither would Junior. In fact, the only person they almost listened to was her.

"Junior, go to the window and get a couple of sodas, and don't mess with any of these people." Kera needed a moment alone with Pain.

"I spoke to your mom today. She wants to come and see you, but I gave her your message even though I think that you are dead wrong for not wanting her to come," Kera said, looking her man in his eyes.

"Baby girl, what you don't understand is that you should leave it alone. Right now, we both are mourning the loss of Kevin. I don't even want to look at myself because, instead of my face, I see my identical twin. It brings me to tears, so the only thing it will do for my moms is make her break down in a state of hysteria. I won't be the cause of that." Pain held his head down as his heart spoke the words of sincerity.

Knowing that Pain was not a sensitive man who wore his feelings on his sleeve, Kera knew that his brother's death was taking an extreme effect on him. It was rare that he would express any form of emotion unless it was related to Junior, but when he did, she felt obligated to be there for him to provide support. This was the man she loved, who had taken care of her since she was 16 years old. She was indebted to him forever.

Holding his hand, she spoke softly. "Daddy, I think you need to at least call her because she needs you more than you can imagine. We all do."

"I'll call later on today to check on her. I just don't want her to travel way down here from New York to end up crying the whole time she's here. Besides, I don't have too much time left in here. When I get out next month, I'll go up there and spend some time with her." Pain looked up to see his son coming back with much more than the sodas he was supposed to be buying.

"This place got more stuff than the corner store around Grandma's way. I ain't never seen The Whole Shebang chips before. These are the bomb!" Junior had a mouthful of chips with crumbs around his face as though he'd stuck his whole head in the bag.

"You see what I have to deal with? He eats everything in sight. Soon we're gonna have to start breeding cattle so we can have enough meat to feed this beast," Kera said, laughing while rubbing Pain's hand that was now draped across her shoulder. She was happy to be around the most important men in her life.

The visit was going great for the three as they talked about future plans. As Junior was talking about being assigned the position of point guard on his school's basketball team, a commotion broke out on the other side of the park.

"Bitch, you ain't coming to see my man!" one of the women yelled out. "Who the fuck are you?"

"First of all, that ain't your man," the other girl replied. "That's my baby daddy."

Before any of the guards had a chance to get to them, the two women started swinging at each other. From what Pain could make out, one had blond locks and the other had curly tracks in her hair. He could tell they were tracks because half of them got thrown to the floor when the woman with blond locks snatched her up and swung her by her hair, causing most of the pieces to fly out everywhere.

Pain could never understand why these guys would never learn to get their visitation straight and not have multiple women show up on the same day. He got that some of these lifers had to have multiple women coming to see them, but what he couldn't get was how they messed up and had them show up on the same weekends. It so happened that these women both had the same man, and he had made the mistake of having them visit at the same time.

One thing about the department of corrections was that in the presence of civilians they would always try to prove they were in control of any situation. Immediately four officers appeared to quickly resolve the situation, which resulted in the two women being escorted off the premises and taken off of the inmate's visitation list. The inmate was taken to confinement, where he would spend at least fifteen days under investigation.

At three o'clock the announcement came over the park intercom telling everyone that visitation was over.

"Well, daddy, I will have the phone back on by tomorrow afternoon, I promise," Kera said while hugging her man, regretting that the time they were spending together had expired.

According to the rules, they were allowed one hug and one kiss upon arrival and departure of all visits. Too much physical contact was strictly prohibited. Some creative inmates would cut holes in their pockets so they could get a quick hand job or whatever else they could get away with while the guards weren't looking. Pain didn't press for any of that. Besides, Kera wasn't the type of girl to freak off in public. She was a good girl until she was in the confines of her bedroom.

After saying his goodbyes, Pain went through the strip-search process to ensure he wasn't bringing contraband into the facility. Walking across the compound, he saw the medical crew rushing an inmate on a stretcher toward the medical building. As they rushed by him, he caught a glimpse of the latest victim of a brutal attack.

"Goddamn, that looked just like Ray-Ray. I wonder who he done pissed off," Pain said to himself as he continued his stride toward the housing unit.

CHAPTER TWO

"Six, ace, five, deuce, four, trey. Yeah!" On one knee, Ray-Ray was on fire as he was picking up all around the board. The dice had been falling his way for about ten minutes straight. The fat kid was one lucky motherfucker and was breaking the whole circle.

Real was smart enough to know who to ride with when it came to betting his money, and this nigga was definitely a payoff. Most niggas liked to roll dice, but Real always got paid off of his side bets, and so far, fat boy Ray-Ray had him up twelve bags of coffee and a whole case of rips. He hadn't even gotten a point yet. His come-out shot was killing the game.

"Y'all bitches tighten up and get that cash right. Hey, broke nigga, you still want your fade, or you wanna call home to get your granny to go bust up her SSI check and hit the Western Union? 'Cause I need my shit on the wood," Ray-Ray taunted Keith while grinning, showing his full twelve-pack.

"Nigga, is you gonna shoot or run your gator?" Keith was in the hole and getting pissed because this nigga's luck was just as annoying as his mouth, which was making him itch to hurry his ass up.

"A'ight, little mama, why don't you kiss these dice for me? 'Cause you sweet as fuck." This nigga Ray-Ray didn't care what came out of his mouth as long as he thought it was funny. "Six, ace, five, deuce, four, trey. Yeah! Point four, little Joe from Kokomo, y'all tighten up twenty more in the main and ten more around the board. I'm trying to break y'all country-ass niggas!" Ray-Ray said while covering bets all around the board.

Usually Real would have had his side bets ready, but his first instinct was to wait for another roll. "Y'all go ahead. I got you on his next point," he said as he winked.

"I thought you niggas up North was about that cash. Tighten up. These niggas is sugar-tank sweet." Ray-Ray's Southern drawl was directed at Real.

"Do your thang, son. I got your next point." Real always went with his first mind.

"A'ight, shawty, it's your cash and your loss. Trey, ace, deuce, deuce, yeah!" Ray-Ray cocked back and tossed the dice. Sure as shit stinks, his luck stood up one more time. "Deuce, deuce. Bitch, better have my money!"

Keith was all in and now he was all out.

"Don't worry, sweet cheeks. If you need a rip or something, I'll let you wash my boxers for three just because you all right with me, princess." Ray-Ray was on top of the world and was using his words to shine on Keith's bad luck.

"Nigga, I said 'hold dice' before you threw that lucky shit. Besides, them shits are kissing." Keith's desperate attempt to stay in the game only made Ray-Ray throw his head back and laugh, preparing to ride his ass.

"What you can do is hold my nuts and kiss my dick, country-ass nigga! Point seen, money lost. You know what the business is." Ray-Ray picked up the last of Keith's chips and held them with previous winnings in his socks, making him look as though he had on two house-arrest ankle monitors. "Who gonna take this nigga's fade while he go check the butt cans for something to smoke?"

Witnessing what was going on, Real could feel a vibe coming from Keith by the look in his eyes. It wasn't toward him but toward Ray-Ray. Things could only get worse, so he stepped to the door of the cell. There were two things about gambling that nobody liked: losing and hearing someone talk shit to you. So the combination of the two could make even a preacher lose religion, and Keith was about to backslide like a motherfucker.

It all went down in five minutes flat. Keith walked to the door and looked down the corridor and turned around with the look of a killer. While Ray-Ray was down on one knee preparing for his next shot, the last words he heard were, "Nigga, steal from me and I'll steal you back!"

With the style of a Serena Williams tennis serve, Keith swung a sock, which concealed a combination lock, at Ray-Ray's head and connected. The impact from the first blow split his head so decently that there was really no need for another, but Keith had a lot on his mind.

"Fuck, nigga, I'll kill you." Keith steadily swung over and over, making the once-all-white sock resemble a candy cane with red stripes courtesy of the blood leaking out of Ray-Ray's twitching body. The words that Keith was saying were incomprehensible, but the aggression in his tone and actions spoke for themselves. Ray-Ray would never roll in another dice game again.

"What's wrong, princess? Ain't shit funny no more, huh? I damn sure don't see you smiling!" The next blow cleared the top six golds right out of Ray-Ray's mouth into the sticky pool of blood on the floor at Keith's feet. "Now that's the winning smile I was looking for!" It was now Keith's turn to laugh, and he had one more laugh to get.

Keith was now looking down and talking to his prey as though they were in a civilized discussion. "You know what, homie? I have to admit, with you winning all my shit and talking all that shit, I was pretty pissed off. I guess I probably took it too hard. I mean, what is a little trash-talking between friends anyway?"

Keith stood up straight and directed his next comment to the audience enjoying the show. While unbuckling his belt, he looked like he was a teacher talking to a classroom. "My niggas, I was dead wrong for being mad earlier, but like me and my boy Ray-Ray just talked about, I was pretty pissed off. But one thing I do know is that it is much better to be pissed off than to be pissed on." A roar of laughter erupted from Keith's mouth as he whipped out his dick and urinated all over Ray-Ray's body from head to toe.

The show was over. Inmates cleared a path by the door while Keith walked out calmly, lighting up a rip as if nothing happened. Real was picking up his winnings while glancing over at Ray-Ray's body barely clinging to life. His chest was slowly moving up and down with an unsteady pace of breathing. He was alive but definitely fucked up.

Real was more than just an inmate. He was a true convict. While others were shocked at the extent Keith went through over a dice game, Real knew that it could have been much worse. The chain gang was not a summer camp for the weakhearted. Shit could pop off in the blink of an eye. This was one of the camps in the Gulf area of Florida where it wasn't uncommon for an inmate to end up in a body bag whether by the hand of an inmate or a member of the prison staff. In order to survive, they had to follow four unwritten rules. One: don't fuck with the TV. Between *Jerry Springer* and football, a motherfucker would get his head split by changing the channel. Two: leave punks alone. Some dudes actually fell in love with these fags and would try to kill you if you even looked in their direction. Three: don't gamble. Ray-Ray was a good enough example. Four: mind your business and don't make anybody's problems your own. When it came down to it, not many would stand in the paint when the shit hit the fan.

"Well, my niggas, this was real, but I'm gonna slide and get my head right," Real said to the remainder of the dice game as he stepped out of the cell. "Ray-Ray, I'll holla at you later when you put yourself back together," he added with sarcasm.

Real hit the yard looking for one thing before he headed back to his cell: the weed man. After five minutes of looking, he spotted the skinny nigga from Tampa who always had the work.

"What happenin', pimpin'?" the skinny inmate said while getting off the dip bar.

"What up, son? I ain't never seen you working out before. What the deal is?"

"Ay, man, you know a nigga about to jump soon, so I got to get ready for them babies out there. I'ma kill them with the tank-top game," Tampa Fifteen said while straining a muscle of his slim arms.

"All right, He-Man, don't hurt nobody, especially yourself. Anyway, you know what I need, so let's handle that." Real was not feeling the hot Southern sun and was ready to head for the dorm.

"I gotcha, cuzo. Let's walk to the T-building and I'll get you right." Fifteen always took his customers through a long walk, which came with an even longer conversation, just to get a sack. He never kept it too close to him in case some officer happened to be watching him too closely. Fifteen was an all-around hustler, and the same rules he gave himself on the street he kept up with in the chain gang.

After about half an hour, Real finally fell off into his cell to find Pain doing his daily workout. Real just shook his head because he knew it was a matter of a minute if not a few seconds before Pain would try to convince him to join in on the workout. Real used to be a gym head before landing in there, but he didn't feel the passion for it anymore. He knew he wasn't in the mood for a workout, but at the same time he knew Pain had a lot on his mind, and Real knew joining his cellmate for a workout would help. Real figured he could do something to help ease some of that frustration his friend was holding on to.

"Y'all niggas kill me with all this working out shit. No matter how big you get, you ain't ever gonna be able to outrun a bullet. And on top of that, the bigger you get, the easier you are to hit," Real joked at Pain just to get his attention.

"Lucky for me, they made more than one gun and a hell of a lot more bullets. Besides, I ain't worried about some fool with a burner," Pain said while getting up off the floor. He had just started his routine.

Working out had become a good outlet for Pain while he did his time. A lot of other inmates did the same thing though, so Pain had to get creative and learn how to do workouts in his cell. Any gym equipment the prison provided was almost always being used by someone.

"So what's up, man? You gonna join me today?" Pain asked his boy. "We can get a decent workout done right now. Sucks there's a shit ton of equipment that I can't use out there, because half these long-term motherfuckers can't give a real nigga an outlet to let some of this steam go."

Real chuckled, listening to his friend complain. "Man, you know all that shit out there is all rusty and no good anyway. Now stop it with all this bitching and complaining. Hurry the fuck up and start doing another set of pushups to warm up." Real chuckled again.

"Yeah, whatever, nigga," Pain said. "Just make sure your fat ass can get three done before dinner." Pain laughed at himself, thinking about Real struggling to do a pushup in the tight cell. Pain got back to the floor to start his second set.

"A'ight, Fat Albert, you up," Pain said when he finished.

Real got in the down position, and as he was pushing up, all he could hear from Pain was, "'One tubby tubby,'" like in the movie *Major Payne*. Real found it so funny that he lost his grip on the floor and fell flat on his face, busting his lip.

"Oh, shit. Oh, shit. Oh, shit!" Pain hollered out in the deepest laugh he'd ever had in his entire adulthood. "Nigga, you just violated yourself! Is your lip okay?" Pain asked as he realized Real had busted his lip.

"Man, fuck you!" Real tried to say like he was mad at Pain, but when it came down to it, that shit was actually funny as hell. Real couldn't help but start laughing as Pain helped him up, which led them both to keep laughing for a minute.

"Fuck me? Nah, I'm not about that life, but you can fuck that weak-ass hand since it can't handle your weight." Pain laughed even harder thinking about it.

Real got up and turned his back to Pain, laughing and knowing he was stuck trying to think of a comeback. That ship had sailed. *How is it that he's always so quick with the jokes when I'm supposed to be the funny one around here?* Real thought.

"A'ight, you got me on that one. Man, I forgot all about that movie. It had that Wayans brother in it, too. That movie was funny as fuck," Real said.

"Now let me do this set for real without you saying some next dumb shit to me." Real got back into his position so he could do his pushups.

He busted out forty and was actually glad that he had agreed to join in on the workout today. When Real stood up, he flexed his biceps, showing Pain he still had it no matter his size. Pain nodded his head in approval. He was glad to be working out and shooting the breeze with his boy, but he wasn't feeling it today.

Real could sense that Pain wasn't really into it. "What's up, man? Why you looking like you lost your cookies on the playground?" Real asked.

"I don't know. It's not the same, you know? I came in here to get a little workout in, and you made it worth the laugh, but fuck! I'm living a life where this shit is as great as it gets. I'm counting the days to when I can get the fuck up out of here and get on with my life. I been missing out on so much while I'm stuck in here, man," Pain said, admitting his raw emotions.

"Man, I know this shit is hard, but we're some strong motherfuckers," Real said, trying to encourage his friend. "Just stay focused and keep your head low like you have been. Your time is coming. Just hang in there."

Pain knew Real was right. He needed to stay focused and be patient. "Yo, my bad, Real. I didn't mean to fuck up the vibe. And you falling was funny as shit, nigga." He laughed, hoping to lighten the mood and change the subject.

Real turned to the mirror and realized that the towel that once covered the mirror was now gone. "Don't tell me my boy is gonna put down his hammers and start dancing on poles in a pair of rhinestone G-strings." Real saw Pain's spirit was returning, so he kept the jokes coming while he took off his prison boots to retrieve his stash. "How was the visitation today anyway?"

"Kera and Junior came to see me, and shit went smooth. Junior is getting big, and his hands are almost as fast as mine. He landed a two piece on me that took me by surprise." Pain was proud of his son and always was willing to let the world know about it.

"So you trying to stay in shape so that little man don't knock you out and show you he is in charge, huh?" Real joked.

"The day that happens, I'll have to cut both his arms off and put them up his little ass. Besides, I taught him everything he knows but not everything I know."

Real climbed up to the top bunk and took out two rolling papers. "Son, watch the door for me while I handle this right quick." Two minutes later the spark of the lighter was followed by the exhale of the light gray mist of calm.

The two bunkies took turns on the joint, exhaling into the exhaust fan and blowing baby powder toward the door to camouflage the smell in case one of the officers decided to get off their lazy asses and actually walk the corridors. By the time the first joint was finished, the plans after their E.O.S. date became the topic of discussion. Besides the fact that they both were from Brooklyn, they both knew how to get money the fast way: strong-arm robbery. Individually, they were a threat to all of the hood-rich dope boys, but together they would soon be a threat to the major connects of the South. That was, if they could maintain the code of honor among thieves if there was such a thing.

CHAPTER THREE

The weed intermission brought some light to the future plans of the city boys with high ambitions. They were in the wrong atmosphere but intended to use it to their advantage. In actuality the best place to find out about criminal connections naturally would come from socializing with criminals. What better place than a penitentiary?

"I'm telling you, that nigga got what we need. Why you think I let him play me close? You know I ain't friendly like that," Real said while lighting up a rip.

"I ain't saying he ain't got it. The question is, can we get all of it without following little buddy around for a month?" Pain knew that Real was a predator when it came down to getting that cash, but his process was slow compared to his. Pain's motto was "Do it big or don't do it at all."

"Listen, man, it ain't gonna take no time at all. I already got everything mapped out to where it is going to be as easy as going to pick up our own cash." Real was ready to show Pain that he was a worthy partner. All they needed was to get on the outside and get the show on the road. In the meantime, he also knew that they would have to develop synchronous thoughts to ensure that every mission would be successfully completed.

Pain didn't want to drift too far off into thought to become too anxious. He had to exercise patience. Besides, the herb was now giving him an urge to eat. "I'll let you do what you do. Right now I'm gonna hit the canteen 'cause I'm hungrier than a motherfucker, and that bullshit they serving in the chow hall ain't gonna do nothing but make me mad."

Getting dressed in his class B uniform of gym shorts, a T-shirt, and New Balance sneakers, Pain grabbed his ID card and headed out to the yard, leaving Real in the cell. The yard was packed with just about everybody trying to hit the canteen. The line was ridiculously long, and there were at least five inmates trying to sell spots. This was the hustle of those who didn't have money sent in from the outside world. Fortunately, Pain had the sense to build a little nest egg while he was on the street. He knew that eventually he would catch a case, so he made sure that he had money for a lawyer, because with one of those public defenders, a man could catch a life sentence for the pettiest crime. Also, before his brother Kevin died in the car accident, he was dropping lump sums of cash in his account from his winnings in street races.

As he merged into the back of the line, the thought of standing and waiting didn't sit well with him. Of the three canteen windows, the only one that he could possibly make it to before the yard closed was the handicap line. He then knew what he had to do. He walked out toward the recreation shed to look for his easy pass.

"What's happening, Bishop?" Pain spotted the old man in the wheelchair and was ready to give his proposition.

Bishop was a cool old coon who was a true convict. He had an E on his ID card, meaning that this was his seventh trip to the chain gang. Due to diabetes, he had to have his left leg amputated and his eyesight was fading as the days went by. "You see it, New York. Just watching these fools on TV. There ain't no way in hell I'm finna go on no *Jerry Springer* and let some whore tell me she really is a man. I'll break my other foot off in her, his, or whatever's ass!" Shaking his head, Bishop continued, "How you gonna be dating some *thing* for months, introducing this thing to your family and friends, and you don't know if it's got a pussy or a dick that's bigger than yours? That's why when I trick with dem whores, the first thing I do is grab that pussy!"

Pain couldn't help but laugh. "Pop, you gonna catch a case going around grabbing people's daughters by the twat. Keep it up, them crackas got a place to hide your ass."

"What the fuck I care about a case? I'm a State-raised baby. Besides, I ain't bullshitting. Them motherfuckers is stupid as hell and probably are punks them damn selves. I don't care what a bitch say. Ain't no woman gonna suck your dick for six months without getting her pussy poked." Bishop was ready to preach on and on about Sodom and Gomorrah, but time was running down for Pain to hit the canteen.

"Look, I need to borrow your wheels to get to the canteen, Pop. Since you ain't doing nothing, how about we take a ride?" Pain's stomach was doing most of the talking now, while his mind was wondering if Real still had some more of the good weed for later on. It actually brought him down to a calmer state of mind.

"Yeah, we can ride, but don't think it's for free! Me and you is all right, but an old man can't make no turd off of friendship." Bishop released the wheelchair brake and pulled a cigarette out of his pocket.

Bending the corner, they came to the line for the third window. They were eighth in line. "I can see why you got in this line. Looks like they must be giving away pussy in this motherfucker!"

"If I weren't so damn hungry, I damn sure wouldn't be out here period. What you want me to get you out the window anyway?" Pain knew Bishop didn't get cash and probably could use some food, cigarettes, and hygiene items. Usually he would offer one of the other cripples two packs of cookies or a pack of cigarettes, but Bishop had a good vibe and was always dropping some knowledge on a brother in his own bizarre way.

"I'll let you know when we get up there, youngblood. Just remember I ain't no cheap date." Bishop flashed his dentures at Pain. "By the way, I heard about the loss of your brother. I'm sorry. Were you guys close?"

"We were twins and as close as it gets. Who told you anyway?" Pain knew only Real knew about it because he never spoke of his family to other people. He didn't even keep pictures.

"Your bunkie. What's his name? Steal?"

"You mean Real." Pain couldn't help but laugh as he corrected the old man.

"Real, Steal, Twenty Cents, Dollar Bill, Nickel Bag. All you jitterbugs got these names besides the ones your mama gave you. Besides, he looks like he'll steal something anyway."

"Real's good peoples. Just another man struggling to make a dollar out of fifteen cents."

"But whose fifteen cents did he steal?" Bishop had a rebuttal for any argument that came his way. "How did your brother die if you don't mind me asking?"

The question took Pain off guard because even though he knew details of the incident, he hadn't spoken them aloud to anyone yet. It was like telling someone about a nightmare he couldn't wake up from. Taking a deep breath, he began to let the words out for the first time.

"Kevin. His name was Kevin," Pain started to explain. "He always was a speed demon when it came to driving. He was one of the best drivers I've ever seen. Anything on wheels he would push to the limits and beyond. Eventually he got into street racing and was pulling in cash off his bets."

"You mean to tell me he was like that boy in *The Fast and the Furious?*" Bishop could see a mist growing in the Brooklyn boy's eyes.

"Shit, Kevin would leave them crackas broke if they ever tried him on that racing tip," Pain said proudly, remembering how Kevin used to stunt on his competition.

"What happened at the end? Don't tell me he got killed because someone didn't want to pay a couple of dollars."

"Naw, not like that at all. He died doing what he loved the most: racing. A car club out of Bushwick put five thousand dollars on one of their drivers against Kevin. They picked one of the most infamous death traps in Brooklyn: the Jackie Robinson Parkway. There are nothing but hairpin turns on the interborough parkway that have caused countless accidents. Well, Kevin was doing his thing in his 2007 BMW M3, his new toy, when he and his competition collided into the side rails. Both drivers were killed instantly."

Bishop watched the Brooklyn boy tell the story and could see the pain in his eyes. "Youngblood, I hope you find a way to see that your brother is in a better place now. Don't let the end of your brother's life mean the end of yours. Just know that you got an angel watching over you now."

"I know. I'm gonna need all the help I can get when I get back out there in the real world." Pushing Bishop up to the window, Pain was ready to order.

After ordering his food, Pain took Bishop back to the rec shed where the TV was on another talk show. "This is another show I can't understand. How these whores don't know who their baby daddy is? Hell, Maury is probably the daddy. You know he be smashing dem whores," Bishop said as he took a bite out of the cheeseburger that Pain bought for him.

"Pop, I'm gonna head back to the dorm and chill. I'll holla at you later." Pain gave the old man some dap and spun around to leave. As he was walking, he thought about the words Bishop told him. He knew that if there was a place called heaven, Kevin would definitely be there. The only thing was, when it was all said and done for him, would they end up in the same place?

Back in the cell, Pain found Real reading *The 48 Laws of Power*. The brother was not only street and chain-gang smart, but he was book smart, too. There was an old saying that went, "The best way to hide something from a black man is to put it in a book." Real wanted to know every secret that these crackas wanted to hide, and he encouraged every brother to do the same.

"You've been reading that book for about two months now. When you gonna finish it and put it down?" Pain said, tossing the cold-cut sandwich, soda, and chips that he brought for his roommate on the bed next to him.

"This ain't no Terry Woods book, son. You don't read this. You study it," Real said while snatching up the sandwich. "There's some real shit up in here that can help in any situation, especially for what we got planned. Read law number three." Real passed the book to Pain and pointed out the introduction of the chapter.

Picking up the book, Pain was shocked to see in black and white what made a lot of sense to him. It was about keeping your moves concealed, so that no one can anticipate what you're doing. If your opponent is kept in the dark, he can't prepare his own moves against you.

"Makes sense, man. Makes a hell of a lot of sense. Most people would think that you're just another ghetto nigga with sticky fingers," Pain said jokingly while tossing the book back to Real.

"That's what I want them to think. That's law number twenty-one. 'Play a sucker to catch a sucker. Seem dumber than your mark.'" Real slid the book right back to Pain.

Pain started to read that passage and heard the words from his roommate. "Besides, I don't steal. I rob. Cowards break in your house when you're not home and steal your DVD player to sell for a rock. I wanna have a motherfucker give me what I want in my hand while I tell them how they got caught slipping!"

A smile crept across Pain's face while he listened to his roommate's testimony. As it turned out, Real would make the perfect partner if his actions proved to be as concrete as his words.

"Man, you a crazy motherfucker!" Pain said in between laughs. "Listen, I'll be back in a few. I need to make a call." Pain got up, stepped into his shoes, and headed out of his cell. Only time would tell if Real and Pain would partner up out in the streets. In the meantime, he had to make a phone call that was long overdue.

***

Half an hour later, Pain realized that spending time on the phone with his mother wasn't as bad as he had expected. She was, of course, mourning the loss of her child, but she seemed to be holding up very well. She was getting a lot of emotional support from her church congregation. One thing about Pain's mother was that she was a God-fearing woman. His oldest memories were of playing with his brother in the church building or playground. His mom would spend every Sunday and at least two weeknights at the church. She'd bring him and his brother with her to Sunday services, Bible studies on Tuesdays, and prayer night on Thursdays. His mom's church friends all loved Kevin and Javon since they were shorties running around the basement of the church. When Kevin passed, the church took up a collection to help pay for the hospital bill and for his mom to be able to afford to take some time off to recover from her loss. Also, it turned out that the street-racing team Kevin was affiliated with paid for the entire funeral expense and much more.

Bewildered, Pain remembered the words that his mother had just told him on the phone. "The Chinese boy your brother used to work in the garage with all the time called me over to the shop to show me something the other day." His mother's voice had sounded enthusiastic when giving the news.

"What was it? You don't know anything about cars, and I've never even seen you drive before," Pain said, knowing his mother could drive but hated dealing with the hectic New York City traffic.

"Boy, I can do everything that y'all can except I don't get in trouble for it." The truth was Mama Phillips was an old-school hustler. She meant it by saying that she did everything from selling weed to robbing some sucker who thought that she was just another vulnerable female. Although she had many male friends, she never dated or brought any men home. One thing about her was she was very particular about who she brought to the place where her twin boys lived. She had a rule about only allowing trustworthy individuals to enter where she and her babies laid their heads to rest at night. That was one rule of many that she never broke. Since the boys' father wasn't around, she wanted them to see that she could hold her own and they should never underestimate the power of a woman. After the twins were born, Mama Phillips's life completely slowed down. She began going to church a lot more often, started a regular job, and just focused on being a good mom.

"Okay, okay, original gangster," Pain had said, poking fun at his mom. "What did Manix have to show you?"

"It seems that your brother was waiting for his dream car to be shipped to him, and it arrived a week after his accident. Manix, God bless his heart, decided that it will only be right that you get it when you get home."

Stunned, Pain was wondering what the hell his mother could be talking about. "I thought Kevin always wanted the BMW that he already had."

"So did I, but it turns out he had big plans for being untouchable in the streets as far as racing. When I got there, the boy talked about the car for twenty minutes before taking off the cover. He was so excited about it that I expected to see wings on it," Mama Phillips said while letting out a giggle.

"Well, what was it, the new *Knight Rider* car or something?" Pain enjoyed hearing his mother laugh, but at the same time he wanted her to get to the point.

"Child, the way he described this car it makes KITT look like a go-kart. He said it had this thingamajig and a lot of other whatchamacallits, and finally I had to almost take off my belt to get him to remove the cover."

"Well, what was it?" Pain was losing patience now and wanted to either know or stop talking about it.

"I had to write it down because I would never remember all those numbers and stuff. I have it written right here in my bag. Here it is. A Mine's R34 skyline GT-R," Mama Phillips recited off the paper.

"Never heard of it. What is it, some kind of military project?" Pain joked while thinking about the mystery car.

"Baby, I have never seen anything like it with all the gadgets and lights Manix wants to add to it. Another thing that shocked me was the steering is on the right side of the car. It is straight out of Japan. Are you even going to be allowed to drive it here in America?"

"I don't know. I never even heard about him ever wanting or having a car coming in," Pain replied. "Guess I'll get more information when I speak to Manix myself."

"Yeah, you're better off speaking to him yourself. Well, I need to get ready to head to sister Migdalia's house." She had sounded a bit sad to be getting off the phone. "As much as I want to stay talking to you, I'm in charge of bringing coffee and my famous blueberry muffins to our girls' night. These ladies would not forgive me if I didn't show up!"

"Oh, no. We can't let that happen!" Pain exclaimed. "How will they ever survive without your homemade blueberry muffins?" he teased.

"Boy, you lucky I can't snuff you through this phone." Pain's mom giggled on the other end. "You're never too old for me to put some hands on you! These hands aren't used just for praying and cooking, you know," she had jokingly threatened her son.

"All right, Ma. Well, you go have a good night with your girls. I love you."

"Love you too, son."

Now as Pain lay in his bed, he was looking forward to speaking with Manix and getting to see the car his brother left to him. On the other hand though, Pain couldn't help but wonder what other stuff his brother had going on that he didn't know about. He and his brother always told each other everything. It didn't make sense that he wouldn't tell him about a special-order car coming in. It was things like this that reminded Pain why he had to do everything in his power to not get locked back up after he got out this time. He hated being stuck on the inside and not being able to get all the intel of shit going on out in the real world. His release day couldn't come soon enough.

CHAPTER FOUR

"I'm telling you he can't fuck with Wayne. The nigga is a lyrical genius!" Fifteen said with a passion.

"The nigga ain't no genius. He got lyrics, but my nigga T.I.P. is the king of the motherfuckin' South, undisputed," spat back J-Ville. This debate over hip-hop's finest was as everyday as breakfast. It always brought out every critic of hip-hop music within earshot.

"First off, the nigga Wayne is raw, but don't forget the cat Gillie, the kid who said Wayne was spitting shit that he wrote for him. Besides, right now that young nigga Pliers is one of the hottest things out there," another voice said, stepping up to add his two cents.

"Yeah, he hot, but fucking with Pliers, a nigga will catch a life sentence. Now the nigga Jeezy will let you know how to get that paper." Fifteen waved down Real to come and put his comment in the debate. Everyone knew that Real was a hip-hop fanatic and would keep it real.

"New York, who you think is the best lyricist out there?" J-Ville said, beating Fifteen to the punch.

Real swaggered over to the group on the yard while pulling on a lit cigarette. He gave dap to Fifteen and nodded toward the others. Normally he would steer away from these conversations, but since he had plans for Fifteen, he had to be friendly for now.

"Y'all niggas still with this same old bullshit? Y'all act like them niggas sending cash to your account or something." Real took the last drag off his cigarette, then threw it to the ground. "Besides, lyrically, since Biggie and Pac, ain't nobody really talking about shit."

The agreement within the circle was unanimous, but J-Ville didn't want to let it go that easily. "Cuz, you just hating on the South since New York ain't producing nothing worth shit anymore."

One thing Real couldn't stand was some country-ass nigga who never crossed the state line talking shit about his city. "First of all, son, it all started in New York. Check the facts. My niggas are all some grown-man shit right now and are making major paper. If y'all want, I guarantee they will step up," Real said, looking J-Ville in the eye. "Matter of fact, the two highest-paid rappers of 2007 are out of New York. Jay-Z is number one, then 50 Cent, and then Diddy."

"Shit, T.I. is paid. What the fuck are you talking about?" J-Ville threw back.

"Yeah, the nigga is paid, but he ain't seeing the cash them boys are seeing. Don't get me wrong, right now the South is the hottest thing on the map, but things can change quick." Real knew that right now the South was in control of the rap game, and only a fool wouldn't admit it.

"Now you talking with some sense. Ain't nobody up North can hold a mic to us down here." J-Ville took Real's last statement for a victory and felt as though he were waving a white flag. "50 was nothing but a hype who ain't talk about shit. His only track that was decent was 'Many Men,' and the rest ain't saying nothing. Dre wasted a million dollars on that clown."

Real could see that J-Ville was not letting go of the argument, so he came to him with facts he couldn't deny. "Rappers are out to get cash. If catering to the public by making songs for the clubs and chicks is going to get you paid, why the fuck not? When he was underground, he and G-unit were touching everything and everybody. Dre made a smart investment with 50. That million came back to him fifty times and better. You keep talking about 50, but I guarantee your ass was playing his shit in that beat-up Chevy you always talking about."

Fifteen broke out laughing at the way J-Ville's face looked after Real gave him the facts that he obviously couldn't deny. Deciding to add fuel to the fire, he asked Real, "Who you think can compete with T.I. and Wayne and Jeezy?"

Off the top of his head, Real spit out a few names that made sense. "Shit, you got Jadakiss, Busta, Jay-Z, Nas. Hell, we got niggas for all y'all best rappers. Lil Wayne is a damn good free stylist, but so is that white boy Eminem."

"Nigga, you crazy as fuck!" J-Ville didn't like the comment but knew inside that both the artists were notorious for their incredible freestyle ability.

The debate continued without resolution for about ten more minutes before Real decided it was time for him to slide, but he needed to holla at Fifteen before the yard closed. Tapping him on the shoulder, he signaled for him to walk with him.

"What up, cuzo? I knew you ain't burn up all that green already," Fifteen said while pulling a rip out of his top pocket.

"Just had to get away from them fools over there. They busy worrying about what another brother's pockets are looking like while their shit is all fucked up. I'm surprised that you even got caught up in that bullshit. That's the only reason I even opened my mouth." Real was ready to get more important matters on the table.

"I'm just trying to pass time to kill these two weeks I got left in this bitch." The thought of hitting the streets put a smile on the Tampa boy's face. He could feel the comfort of his ostrich-skin car seats under him and the babies who would love to ride on the twenty-eight-inch rims.

"I feel you. I'll be right behind you. After you leave, I've got less than a month, and so does my man Pain. I'm gonna pass through Tampa to see them babies you claim is so fine running around there." Real wanted to see something, but he really wasn't as interested about the females as he was concerned with the free money he could get out there on the strength of a nigga who just wasn't as strong as they thought.

"I told you, all you got to do is get at me and I got you. That's my town and them hoes know it." Fifteen was a little cocky, but he was right. His name rang bells from Georgia to Miami. He was connected to some *chicos* who had major weight. They practically gave away bricks for nothing compared to the twenty grand that was the common price unless you had a serious connect. Real was planning to get at him just to get at the *chicos*.

"We'll see. I'm definitely gonna pass through, but a nigga gotta get straight with my cash flow first." Real had cash stashed away to do just about anything he pleased, but he wanted to play his card under the table to see how friendly Fifteen would be.

"Listen, I got you for whatever. Like I said, it's my town, so it's my treat. I'm gonna show you how we do it down in the South. I'll pick you up at the gate and hook you up with whatever." Fifteen admired the swagger of Real and had plans for him also. Once he showed him how he ran things on the street, he would have no problem having Real go up to New York to find some buyers so he could expand his marketing area.

"You got a good talk game, little man, a hell of a talk game. You sure you ain't from Brooklyn?" Real joked with Fifteen. "I'm definitely gonna holla at you for that VIP treatment, but right now a nigga hungry as a motherfucker. I'm gonna hit the canteen before they close the yard." As the two headed toward the canteen, two words went through both of their minds: *got him*.

After the 9:30 master roster count, Pain and Real sat in their cell talking about the streets of Brooklyn and the places they'd been. Although the two never crossed paths on the streets, they shared a few memories like the infamous weed spots in Flatbush and Bushwick, going to the Tunnel night-club in Manhattan, and hanging out in Wingate Park on Monday nights for the free concerts. After talking for about an hour and a half, Real pulled out the remaining sack of weed that he got from Fifteen earlier in the day.

"Dawg, what you got, a weed dispenser in your shoe or something?" Pain got up to check the door to make sure the hallway was clear of any officers so his roommate could roll up the joint. Although he wasn't a fiend for smoking, the talk of home made him feel like he was back on the block, so why not act like it?

"You know I always keep one in the chamber for when the urge hits." Real stuck two sheets of rolling papers together, preparing to roll the joint. Within a minute the stick was rolled and was ready to be fired up. "Get the baby powder and put the towel under the door." The spark of the lighter illuminated the room for a brief second, revealing a shadow that didn't belong.

From outside the window a voice shattered the calm vibe the roommates had planned, followed by the blue beam of a flashlight. "All right, Cheech and Chong, let me see your hands and don't move!" the CO barked through the window, grabbing his radio off the side of his belt.

Real's mind went into overdrive. He knew he had a decision to make that really didn't take too much thought: either spend sixty days in confinement for the possession of cannabis in a state facility—plus another sixty days, because they would definitely be given a piss test when they got to the box—or spend thirty days for disobeying a verbal order. He chose the latter. Looking the officer in the face while he radioed for another to come to the room for assistance, Real balled up the joint and swallowed it. Pain remained cool as a fan and dusted the powder off his hand and picked up the towel from under the door.

Seconds later the cell door swung open, and another redneck rushed in the room to find the two roommates calmly standing there, attempting to look innocent to all accusations. "What the fuck's going on in here?" He stared the two men in the face, trying to intimidate the fearless duo. "Answer me, boy!"

"Boy swung from the trees with Tarzan, and he damn sure ain't in this room!" Pain didn't like the out-of-shape redneck and didn't let his "good ol' boy" attitude intimidate him.

"Don't sass me, inmate. I asked you a goddamn question!" The officer analyzed the situation around him. He stood five feet eight inches in a room with two inmates who showed no fear. He looked at Pain's six-foot-three frame along with Real's six-foot-two frame and realized that if things got physical, he could not win. "Let's see what the lieutenant has to say about your smart mouth. Turn around and cuff up!"

"Naw, you ain't cuffing nobody in here up! You better call the LT down here, 'cause we ain't did shit!" Real voiced while taking off his shirt. Although he wasn't a workout fanatic, he was naturally muscular, and his tattooed skin made him look like a beast.

While the redneck officer stood there looking confused, Sergeant Wellman walked into the room. She was an older black woman who treated inmates with the same manner as she would her own grandchildren, and because of that the inmates respected her. "Phillips and Brown, what's all the ruckus about? I'm ready to go home and you guys are giving my officers a hard time." Sarge walked up to where Real stood, her hand on her hip.

"Sarge, we ain't did nothing. Your officers must be bored or something." Out of respect, Real tried not to curse around Wellman. Talking to her was like talking to Grandma. "I ain't gonna let them handcuff us and end up being a punching bag in the mop closet."

"Okay, okay, calm down. I'll take you to the LT's office myself, but first let that air out of your chest and put your shirt back on before I take you in the mop closet myself." Sarge knew that the white officers did indeed trap up inmates and would beat them up just for sport, but it wasn't going down like that tonight. She handcuffed Pain and Real, dismissing the second officer. The officer in the window and Sarge walked the men to the lieutenant's office.

In the lieutenant's office, the air conditioning was on full blast, and everything was neatly in place. The first thing Pain noticed was the infamous pickle jar that was filled with gold teeth that were once worn by inmates who thought they were tough enough to challenge the department of corrections. The one thing these crackas hated was that, while they worked ten-hour shifts every day to make enough to pay their bills, dope boys made quick money on the streets and could wear enough gold in their mouths to pay for their trailers for a couple of months. Neither Pain nor Real wore gold teeth, so at least they didn't have to worry about getting emergency dental work.

Frustrated and ready to go home to his fat wife and disobedient kids, the lieutenant listened to the officer's statement of why the men were in his office this late at night. "If they were smoking weed, where is it?" the lieutenant barked at the officer.

"Sir, I . . . I believe he swallowed it. I was outside the window." The officer was stuttering and inconsistent with his words. "I told him not to move, but he didn't listen."

"Shit, I can't blame him. You were standing outside the window like some goddamn cat burglar. Why didn't you just go in the room and get some concrete proof?" Real listened to the lieutenant bark at the officer and tried his best to hold a straight face.

"I . . . I didn't think . . ." Before the officer could finish, the lieutenant slammed his fist on the desk, causing everyone in the room to jump.

"I know you didn't, but I guess you think I'm going to walk behind some inmate and wait for him to shit out some dope!" Now standing, the lieutenant was red in the face with disgust of the poor performance of the officer.

"We could always give them a urinalysis," the officer suggested in a childlike whisper, trying to reestablish credibility.

"That's what's wrong with you young cocks. You think just because you pass some test to become an officer you know everything. Let me tell you, I've been in the system for twenty years, and I know that we could piss test them right now and they will probably come out cleaner than you and me. Hell, an inmate can take a piece of newspaper and two tubes of toothpaste and make a blade that will cut you clean in half!" The lieutenant then turned to Real and Pain, who stood there looking straight ahead, trying not to show any emotion.

"Being that my staff doesn't have any concrete proof on you punks and it is almost midnight, I'm gonna spare your narrow asses. Sarge tells me that you aren't troublemakers, so I don't expect y'all to make her out to be a liar. I'm going home to deal with this fat bitch and my bad-ass kids, and I don't feel like doing any paperwork, but if I see either of you in my office again, I'm going to add them pearly whites to that jar over there. Do I make myself clear?"

"Sir, yes, sir!" the two men said in unison, glad to be spared.

Back in the cell, the two Brooklyn boys shared a laugh over the recent events. Minutes later the shift changed, and the new officers walked by, doing a quick head count. After they passed, Real reached down to his boot and came up with a little package. Pain looked and shook his head and laughed.

"I told you I always keep one in the chamber for when the urge hits. Besides, one monkey don't stop no show." Real prepared to roll the joint, and then turned to Pain. "This time check the window."

CHAPTER FIVE

During the last stretch of his sentence, Pain sat back and spent his time meditating on his future plans for when he hit the streets. He was aware that a lot had changed during his forty-eight-month incarceration period except for one thing: the power of the pistol. He had to make moves and make them strong, or else he was destined to watch the world from the point of view of a loser. He made mental notes of his soon-to-be victims and the kind of cash they had at their disposal. The last thing he wanted was drugs. That involved double hustling himself, and he was not about to try moving some product when he could sit back and wait for them to do all of the work.

His mind raced to the Africans in Atlanta. These clowns couldn't speak English but had major connections that made them the second-strongest distributors of cocaine and weed in comparison to the infamous Black Mafia Family. Realistically Pain knew that going up against the B.M.F. would be suicide because their soldiers were more dedicated than the followers of bin Laden, but the Africans were touchable, very touchable.

Suddenly his thoughts were interrupted by the voice of his cellmate.

"Son, you got to see this shit that's about to go down," Real said while laughing. "These two clowns are squared off about to fight, and both of them look scared to death."

Not really interested, Pain turned to Real. "Who? I ain't about to watch no catfight. Shit, I could probably see a better match on *Jerry Springer*."

"Naw, man, *Springer* ain't got shit on the funny shit that's about to go down. It's them niggas Ray-Ray and Keith. They right there at the handball court." Real motioned over his shoulder toward the two amateur gladiators in their concrete ring.

Looking over his shoulder, Pain could see that his partner was right. Even in the confined space of the handball court there was enough space between the two so-called fighters to park an Escalade truck. They were definitely scared to bump heads, but both were trying to save face. Also, Pain noticed that the two guards out there were Officers Tompkins and Pearlman. Neither of the two would break up a fight. It was all entertainment for them.

Taking a seat on the bleachers, Pain and Real were ringside at the main event. Smoking a cigarette, Real let out a number of laughs at the tongue wrestling contest that was going on. "These clowns would scare a nigga over the phone, but neither one of them gonna kill nothing and ain't gonna let nothing die," Real said loud enough, trying to provoke some action to start.

"Fuck-nigga, you had to steal me to whup me. My back ain't turned now, fuck-boy. Whassup!" Ray-Ray barked, realizing the group was slowly growing larger. Included in that group were a large number of inmates from his hometown of Duval County. In the chain gang, it was an advantage to have the support of your home team in case things got hectic. Whether you knew them from the streets or not, they would ride with you to let everyone know that your town ain't to be fucked with.

Keith, seeing that his hometown team of Daytona was just as thick as the Jacksonville boys, was more eager to get the fight going, except one thing told him to be cautious. He couldn't see Ray-Ray's right hand. He stalled him out by circling toward his own left to attempt to get a better view of what Ray-Ray could be hiding. "My nigga, I already know you got a mouthpiece on you, but do you got hands to go with it? Besides, ain't you got a dental appointment to get them partials put in?" Keith continued to taunt his adversary, remembering the day in the cell when Ray-Ray used that same slick rap to provoke him. Besides, he was waiting for the right moment to catch him off guard so that he could get a lead on the situation. Getting the first blow in would give him better control over the situation.

Just like a crowd at amateur night at the Apollo, the spectators who were now tired of hearing the monologue of the two started to stir shit up with words of their own.

"What y'all gonna do, fuck or fight?" a voice from the crowd yelled, adding to the tension that already grew within the handball court.

Ray-Ray glanced toward the crowd, thinking back to the day he got pissed on.

Pain, getting tired of sitting there watching nothing, wanted to get up and smash Ray-Ray for even hesitating to handle his business. There was no way in hell he should even have to think twice about trying to beat the shit out of Keith. If it were his situation, Keith would have been dealt with quickly.

"This nigga Ray-Ray has got to be the dumbest motherfucker in captivity!" Pain heard Real say with a tone of disgust. "There is no way Keith would be able to say a slick word out of his mouth. On sight I would have split his shit wide open, ain't no rapping!"

"Bro, I was thinking the same shit. The way you told me he got pissed on, shit! I would have to catch him, whup him, and then shit in his mouth, and of course I'd have to make sure his grill was as fucked up as mine by putting these boots to good use." Pain's words were then followed by a sharp cry of pain.

Apparently Keith thought his opponent was distracted for a moment, so he lunged forward, only to get the surprise of his life. Ray-Ray had a custom-made shank concealed in the right sleeve of his sweatshirt, courtesy of his *chico* homeboy Juan. The first hit punctured Keith in his abdomen area, causing a shrilling cry that alerted everyone around. The jagged edges of the chain gang–crafted buck-knife had a deadly effect.

Standing on the bleachers, Pain could see all that was happening. What he witnessed was gruesome slaughter that appeared to be in slow motion. As Ray-Ray pulled the blade out of a devastated Keith, Pain could see death in the face of the Daytona boy. Along with the blade, an object that looked like a blood-soaked hamburger came out of the Daytona boy's stomach and just seemed to hang from his guts. The second hit was delivered with such force right below the rib cage that blood erupted from Keith's mouth before he fell to the pavement.

Witnessing the horrific act, Officers Tompkins and Pearlman made their way cautiously toward the crowd in an attempt to cause them to disperse. Pearlman radioed in for a medical unit while Tompkins unsnapped his Mace canister and pressed his panic button. Things were about to go down, and Pain didn't want any part of it.

"Show's over, man. Let's go!" Pain suggested to Real. It sounded like a command from an army drill sergeant.

Keeping an eye on the events taking place, Real got off the bleachers and started toward the dormitory with Pain when a group of officers came rushing on the scene. He then spotted Fifteen, who evidently had enough sense to leave the area. "Hey, big man, what you up to?" Real said to Fifteen as he met him at the gate.

"Ain't nothing, cuzo. Them fools about to get the whole pound locked down over that shit. I'm down to a day and a wake-up. I don't need any drama, cuzo." Fifteen's words were accompanied by his constantly looking around his perimeter. "I was looking for you earlier to give you something before I left."

Camouflaged in the form of a handshake, Fifteen handed a thick piece of paper to Real. "What this is, son?" Real inquired while sticking it in his pocket.

"Just my info for when you about to leave, cuzo. Have somebody give me a call, and I'll be at the gate when you get out." Fifteen flashed his six-pack smile.

"Dawg, that's straight, but I told you before, I got to get my cash right first. I ain't trying to be no leech." Real was once again testing the waters to see if this fish would bite.

"Cuzo, I got you!" Fifteen said loud and clear to emphasize the sincerity of his words.

Suddenly someone came frantically running by with a long object in his hand. "Get out of my way!"

It was Ray-Ray. Somehow, he managed to evade the squad of officers and ran toward the gate in hopes of getting God knows where. He was a trapped animal in a cage and didn't know it. Worst of all, he still had a weapon in his hands.

Reaching the blacktop of the compound, Ray-Ray stopped briefly to analyze his situation and realized he had no wins. It seemed as though security personnel was multiplying by the second, all focused on him standing there with a bloody dagger in his grip. Feeling like a quarterback caught up in a blitz play, Ray-Ray scrambled, trying to find a break in the defensive line and hoping not to get sacked. Swinging the blade wildly, Ray-Ray knew that he was up against all odds that would only lead to never seeing the free world again.

"I didn't do nothing. Why y'all fucking with me? Y'all got the wrong guy! This ain't even my knife. I just found it!" Ray-Ray's desperate attempt to give an alibi wasn't making sense to himself. He asked himself why he had not thrown the knife away instead of running with it. It was an all-around bad situation that could only get worse.

"Drop the weapon, inmate!" an officer ordered while the others got into blitz formation. "Don't make things harder on yourself than necessary!"

"I told y'all it wasn't me!" Ray-Ray continued to deny the act he'd committed, not noticing the two rookie officers creeping up from the rear. He was focused on the squad in front of him until the expression on Sergeant Radcliff's face changed and a command erupted from his mouth.

"Fall back! Fall back!" the sergeant barked.

Hearing the words from the sergeant's mouth, Ray-Ray tried to register what he could be talking about. Just then he felt an impact from behind, causing him to fall forward to the ground. By reflex, he tried to break his fall with his hands, but unfortunately he still had the blade tightly gripped.

Rookie Officer Jenkins, seeing that the inmate was focused on the officers in front of him, decided to apprehend Ray-Ray by tackling him to the ground in hopes of cuffing him up. This would show his superiors that he was a good addition to the security personnel. He heard the sergeant telling him to fall back, but he was already in motion and could not stop. Now lying on top of the inmate, he realized that the man who was just violently swinging a blade and screaming incoherently was now strangely still. Getting up slowly, he braced his hands on Ray-Ray's back to prepare to secure him with handcuffs when he noticed a heavy pool of blood developing under him.

"You stupid son of a bitch! Who the fuck told you to do that dumb-ass cowboy bullshit?" The sergeant was now red in the face, screaming at the rookie while shoving him to the side to get to Ray-Ray. "Alert the medical unit now! We can't lose two in one day!"

"Sir, I was just trying to end the standoff as quick as possible. He was swinging that shank and posing a threat." The rookie was explaining that he was trying to do the right thing.

Ray-Ray fell on the blade, piercing his heart and causing blood to flow from the wound and from his mouth. His body made one final spasm while he soiled his pants with urine and shit. Now lying on a stretcher back at the handball court, Keith's body went through the same final spasm only two minutes earlier. The inmate population was now decreased by two.

"Get these inmates to their housing units now!" Holding his head in frustration, the sergeant yelled into his walkie-talkie. "Look at this shit. One day away from the regional inspection, and we've got two dead bodies!"

"All inmates, immediately report to your assigned housing areas! All inmates, immediately report to your assigned housing areas," sounded from the PA system throughout the compound.

CHAPTER SIX

As a result of Ray-Ray and Keith's final standoff, the compound was locked down for two days. Officer Jenkins was suspended from duty indefinitely, and the regional inspection included a lot of ass chewing because of the two civil lawsuits being filed against the institution for liability. A few inmates were asked to make statements on the deadly situation, and among those few was inmate Rashan Brown, aka Real.

Just like the others, Real was briefed by the lieutenant on what to say with a promise of getting two months deducted from his sentence, which would make his out date the same as Pain's. Even though he had no love for the crackas whose jobs were at stake, he had an opportunity to get out earlier, so he jumped on it.

Fifteen was released from prison during the time the compound was locked down. Real made sure he held on to the number that he left because he believed that Fifteen was definitely going to be his come-up. Along with his number and address,

Fifteen also left Real with a little more than a quarter ounce of weed so he could have something to meditate on, because he also believed Real was going to be his come-up.

Five days before their release date, Pain was working out in his room when his cellmate came in with his radio on his head singing the hook to D.J. Khaled's "I'm So Hood." Pain noticed that the back of Real's blue shirt had damp reddish brown spots that looked a lot like blood. He already knew that it could have only come from Real's chain-gang passion for tattoos.

"What's the new piece looking like?" Pain asked his partner as he got up from his last set of push-ups.

Pulling off his radio, Real smiled, saying, "I got the back piece that fits perfectly with what's about to pop off when I hit the streets." He then took off his shirt and turned his back toward Pain to expose the fresh artwork.

Beneath the small spots of blood, Pain could see the bizarre picture that only Real would get. Covering his back was an angel dropped down on his knees, crying with his broken wings in his hands. The fallen angel appeared to be shouting toward a light from heaven, and on the top of the picture was a caption that Pain recognized from the Bible: "*Eli, Eli, Lama Sabachthani?*" It was definitely an original piece.

"Those were the last words Jesus said on the cross before the earth began to tremble. It's Hebrew for—" Real tried to explain the caption but was interrupted by Pain.

"'My God, my God, why have you abandoned me?'" Pain finished his roommate's statement to let him know that he also knew the Bible.

"I know you can speak Spanish fluently, but I ain't know that you knew anything about Hebrew." Real looked surprised that Pain understood the caption on his back.

Pain was indeed fluent in Spanish because Kera was Puerto Rican, and she taught him over the many years they were together. It came in handy, especially in the chain gang. A nigga had to be careful around the *chicos*. They could be plotting to slash your throat with a lawnmower blade. Pain made sure that when they started speaking Spanish around him, he was aware of what was being said.

"Naw, I don't speak Hebrew, but I have read the Bible. The piece is straight as hell. He even got the colors up in there." Pain nodded his head in approval. "I might go see him after we go to medical to pick up the results of the physical."

Real had mixed emotions about the prerelease physical. He was naturally happy that he was at the point in his bid where the word "release" was involved, but the physical included the most feared subject to any promiscuous person in the world: an AIDS test. Upon entering the prison system, every inmate was tested for the virus to determine what facility they'd be sent to. Real's result on his initial test was nonreactive, which put his mind at ease. Although he did not mess with any of the punks on the compound or any of the female officers who would secretly give up some pussy to a select inmate they felt could keep a secret, he couldn't help but think of all the females he had in the past and pray that they were as clean as they appeared.

"Man, I hope these crackas don't keep us up at medical all day with that bullshit," Real grumbled out to mask his paranoia of possibly getting bad news.

"Stop your fussing. You ain't got shit else more important going on." Pain was just as nervous as his homeboy about his test results even though he knew he was clean.

"Our callout is for three o'clock, so we got about forty-five minutes. I got to go drop off this shit to Bishop, so I'll catch up with you in a minute," Pain said while gathering up two full canteen bags of cigarettes, coffee, soups, and hygiene products. To Real's surprise, a majority of it belonged to him.

"Bro, ain't that my shit you got in there?" Real bent down to his locker to see that it was now empty except for two packs of cigarettes and half a bag of coffee.

"Breathe easy. You don't need this shit no more. I'm giving all this to the old man to hold him down when we leave." Pain didn't even pause from what he was doing. "Besides, for what we gonna get into, we can use all the blessing we can get."

Real felt what his homeboy was saying and had nothing to say on the situation. Most of the stuff that he had was won on the spades, skin, and poker table. *Easy come, easy go, fuck it.*

The day was finally here, and the boys were ready to hit the streets and do their thing. Real contacted Fifteen by having Pain's girl call him so he could come and get him at the gate. That morning, Real woke up to see Pain doing push-ups and decided to get a couple of sets in with him. Pain looked at Real in shock because this was totally out of character for him.

"All right, bro, let's go over this again. You going with wifey, of course, and you want me to contact you in seventy-two hours to get the show on the road," Real said, admiring his frame in the mirror.

Real never worked out, but he was naturally big. Standing at six foot two inches, his caramel skin was covered in tattoos except for his legs. Although he was a handsome man, his facial expressions commanded respect from men. He kept a bald head, which complemented his trimmed beard and mustache. During his time in prison, he was constantly harassed about whether he had a shaving pass.

"Yeah, that's the plan. You sure that nigga Fifteen is gonna come through? You can ride with me." Pain wanted to make sure his boy was going to be straight.

"Bro, I got this. Besides I ain't going to put your wife's plans for you on pause so you can drop me off somewhere. I'll get up with you on schedule." Real went back on the ground to finish another set of push-ups. Anticipation of finally walking through the gate gave him an energy rush that he could barely tame.

At the stroke of seven o'clock, the Brooklyn boys were making their final trip across the compound toward the property room to change from the state-issued blue uniform into their street clothes. As they were walking, they spotted Crazy Harold in his monthly routine to try to get transferred to another camp. The inmate had climbed up to the roof of the chapel and posted up, refusing to come down. He was dressed in a pair of boots, a hat, and a belt, but besides that, he was naked as the day he was born.

"Look at this motherfucker here. At least he didn't climb on that hot-ass kitchen roof this time." Real couldn't help but laugh at the scene. "I can't front, son, I'm gonna miss some of this shit."

"You must be planning on coming back." Pain also was amused by the situation but was more concerned with getting to the parking lot. He couldn't wait to get the hell out and away from this place. Whether he was going to miss it anytime soon or any day in this lifetime was the last thing on his mind right now.

"Hell nah, they can have this shit. Next judge I see will be God Himself!" Real's words came with conviction from the pit of his soul. He was not coming back, at least, not breathing. "Make them kill you, Harold!"

Twenty minutes later Pain was dressed in a pair of black Evisu jeans, a navy blue short-sleeve button-up shirt by Ralph Lauren, and a black tank top with a pair of original tan-colored Timberlands.

Real's E.O.S. package included an authentic Lawrence Taylor throwback jersey, a pair of Rocawear shorts, and a pair of roll-down Timberlands with the left foot rolled down and the right one extended. He also had three bandanas—red, white, and blue—folded up in his pocket. The prison thought they were gang flags, so they wouldn't allow him to wear them on the premises.

On the other side, in the parking lot, was Kera anxiously waiting for Pain to come out. She hadn't been able to sleep all night from how nervous and excited she was. She had spent the last few days cleaning the house top to bottom to make sure everything was perfect for when Pain came home.

She had also gone to get her hair, lashes, and nails done so she could look on point for when she picked her man up. She went to her waxing lady to make sure she was baby smooth and fresh for when they got home. She was positive one of the first things Pain was going to want to do when they got home was have some fun in the bedroom, making up for all the time he couldn't satisfy his woman and give her some loving.

Kera was getting impatient. She kept looking up at the door every time she heard the slightest noise, hoping to see Pain being led out. Finally, after what felt like an eternity of waiting, she saw him exiting through one of the doors behind a fence with some barbwire throughout the top area.

Walking out to the parking lot, Pain was immediately greeted by Kera with open arms and tears of joy.

"Oh, my God, baby. I can't believe you're finally out!" Kera exclaimed between giving her man kisses all over his face. She was thrilled to finally have her man back. She could feel the weight of the world lift off her shoulders as she kissed and hugged him passionately.

"Yes, babe, me too. Can't believe I'm out here." Pain closed his eyes and took a second to take a deep breath in. It had been so long since he'd taken in the smell of fresh air as a free man. What made this even better was having his woman right by his side. As he took a deep breath in, the smell of the fresh outdoors mixed with the smell of Kera's perfume was like a gift from heaven.

"Babe, there's someone I want to introduce you to," Pain said to Kera.

"Oh, okay," Kera replied. She wrapped one of her arms tightly around Pain's left arm as if she were a child being dropped off at the first day of school.

Pain walked over toward where Real was standing so he could formally introduce her to him. Although Pain was not at all a jealous man, he rarely exposed Kera to a lot of people he dealt with. He had a difficult time trusting people, so he always felt it was important to keep his most loved ones to himself just in case anyone ever decided to hurt him through his family. Pain making the decision to introduce his girl to Real was a very big deal. It truly showed that Pain was letting his guard down and considered Real to be a trustworthy friend.

"Nice to meet you. I spoke to your friend, and he said he will be here at eight o'clock like you asked," Kera said as she still held on to her man's arm.

"I appreciate that, Mrs. P. You guys better get going. He still got about ten minutes to get here. Big bro, I'll get up with you in a couple of days. Be safe." Real gave Pain a dap and a quick shoulder hug and headed toward the bench.

"All right, son. If anything happens, hit me up and I'll come scoop you up." Pain walked toward his truck with Kera in tow.

Pain's truck was just as clean as the day he'd left it. In fact, it only had an extra 120 miles on it. The 2003 Chevy Suburban was all black with a tan leather interior, complemented by wood grain paneling with the word "Pain" engraved in gold lettering on the headrests. With eight-inch solar barracks in each door and six eighteen-inch speakers in the rear pushed by class D amps, it was definitely an earthquake while gliding on twenty-eight-inch Lowenhart three-dimensional fans with rubber-band-thin Pirelli tires.

Once he disarmed the alarm system, he watched Kera climb up in the passenger seat and lean back. Walking over to the driver's side, he noticed the two female officers who ran the inside groundwork detail looking in his direction. Many times during his incarceration period these two bad-bodied gold diggers tried to make his time difficult by assigning him to jobs like picking up cigarette butts, sweeping the sun off of the sidewalk, or picking weeds with his hands for hours. Now they were gazing in amazement at his truck and smiling as if they were friends.

As if on cue, Kera stepped out of the truck and walked over to the driver's side and placed around his neck a forty-two-inch platinum chain encrusted with diamonds. The pendant was of Michael the Archangel with diamond wings spread out, and in his hand was a spear with a red diamond for a tip. Kera then opened the door for her man and planted a kiss on his lips. As they pulled out of the parking lot, car alarms were set off as "Hail Mary," the song of hip-hop's most beloved prophet, Tupac, rang out through the speakers.

CHAPTER SEVEN

"So are we getting Junior early from school?" Pain asked Kera as they made their way back into the neighborhood.

"No, baby. He has to stay after school today. The boy caught another detention for showing up late to gym class, and he skipped social studies class, too," Kera explained.

"Oh, man. I'm going to have to speak to him about that. He can't be messing up with school like this." One thing Pain was serious about was making sure his son was getting a good education. He didn't want his son to have a life like his. He always joked around with Junior about stuff, but making sure his son turned out to be a productive member of society was a top priority for Pain. He never wanted him to be running the streets like Pain had been doing since he was a young buck. One thing he never wanted to see was his son behind bars. The only bar he would ever want his son to have to deal with was the bar exam if he ever decided to become a lawyer. Pain doubted his son would ever go into any type of law enforcement though.

"Yes, please talk to him. I'm hoping now that you're coming home, he'll start to act better, because he really has been doing all kinds of crazy things lately," Kera expressed. She hadn't been fully honest with Pain about everything that had been going on at home. The truth of the matter was that Junior had been acting very disrespectful over the last year. Kera wasn't sure if it was a combination of his father being gone along with him being a young teenager, but his attitude had been out of control.

"Don't worry. Things are going to be different now that I'm back," Pain reassured her as they pulled into the driveway.

There was a car he didn't recognize parked in the driveway. He was a little bothered that someone would have the nerve to be parked in the driveway, especially on the day he was set to come home. Nonetheless, he wasn't going to let something small like that ruin his good mood today. It'd take a whole lot more than that to mess up the feel-good vibe he had going on.

"Whose car is this?" he casually asked Kera.

"That car?" Kera asked innocently.

"No, that car parked over there." Pain pointed at a random car parked in front of the neighbor's house. "Yes, that car. The car you just parked behind."

"You'll see," Kera said in a teasing voice.

As soon as they entered the house, Pain's nose was assaulted with a variety of smells. He closed his eyes and took them all in. He could make out the smell of chicken frying in a pan. He could also hear the sound of oil sizzling. There was an underlying smell of something baking in the oven.

"Do I smell fried chicken, baby?" He turned to Kera as he took in the deepest breath he could. "And is that cornbread I smell coming from the oven, too?" Pain sounded like a little boy on Thanksgiving night getting ready for family dinner.

"Not just any fried chicken," Kera responded. Just as she said that, Mama Phillips came walking through the kitchen entryway.

"You didn't think I wasn't gonna be here for my baby boy's homecoming now, did you?" Mama Phillips exclaimed as she walked over to her son and gave him the biggest hug.

"Hi, Ma. So glad you're here," Pain said as he leaned in to give his mom a hug. It was true what they said: no matter how old you got, nothing ever compared to a mother's hug. Pain was grateful to be home.

"Wow, I feel like a true king right now," Pain said. "It feels so good to be home and be surrounded by the two most important women in my life. The only thing that would complete this for me is if Junior were here."

"Don't worry, baby. He'll be here soon enough. Trust me, he wanted to be here too."

"Thank the Lord you are back home safe and sound," Mama Phillips said. "Now let me get back to the kitchen and check on this food. Last thing we want is to be eating burnt chicken." Mama Phillips ran off to the kitchen, leaving Pain and Kera alone in the living room.

"Speaking of eating," Pain whispered teasingly into Kera's ear, "you got something of mine that I've been waiting to eat."

"Oh, do I now?" Kera said as she giggled. "Don't worry. She's all ready for you," she said as she turned and pulled him by the hand to lead him toward the bedroom.

CHAPTER EIGHT

"Cuzo, I told you that your boy was gonna come through for you." Fifteen was lying back on his couch, pouring another shot of Hennessy for himself while his jailhouse friend was on the other couch smoking a blunt of popcorn 'dro.

"Yeah, son, you did that. It's been a while since a nigga got the red-carpet treatment." Real was high as hell but still was focused on his mark. He had three days before he linked up with his partner, and he wanted to produce immediately.

"It ain't over yet, my nigga, it just started. I know you got to holla at your peoples at home, so I gonna let you use my Caddy. Just pick me up at about eleven o'clock tonight, and I'll show you some spots in the city that ain't in the travel brochures." Getting up from the couch, Fifteen walked over to the counter that separated his kitchen from his living room and picked up a set of car keys.

"Dawg, I do got to go check on my shortie. She probably dialing up to the prison to see if they let me go." Real put the remainder of the blunt in the crystal ashtray and peeled himself out of the recliner.

Fifteen led Real through the laundry room to the garage. Turning on the lights, Real saw two cars in the garage—the old-school Impala that Fifteen used to pick him up from prison and the Cadillac. The '73 Impala SS was metallic and black, trimmed with chrome from bumper to bumper with presidential dark-boy tints. Like most of the Southern boys, Fifteen had a passion for big rims but didn't want to go overboard, so he had a lift suspension to accommodate his twenty-eight-inch Dub spinners wrapped in custom Kumho tires. Although the car was older than the Tampa boy, the pioneer touch-screen head unit with the four Rockford Fosgate amps to power the eight ten-inch Rockford Fosgate subwoofers definitely made it Y2K compatible.

"I know you New York boys are used to Lexus, Beemers, and Benzes, but I'm sure you won't mind pushing this old hog for a minute." Fifteen tossed the keys to Real as he pushed the button on the garage-door opener.

"My nigga, as long as this motherfucker has a gas pedal and a steering wheel, I ain't got no complaints." Real let out a chuckle as he walked over to the driver's side of the Cadillac. He looked it over and realized that it was not just any old car. It was another one of Fifteen's auto makeovers. While getting into the car, he damn near hit himself in the chin with the butterfly doors.

It took Real about two hours to get from Tampa to his spot in Apopka. The Cadillac was a smooth ride for an old car. He had to give Fifteen credit for his restoration to the '69 Coupe DeVille because it was running as though it were straight off a showroom floor. Enjoying his long yearned-for freedom and good weather, Real rode with the black Louis Vuitton top down, exposing the black microsuede interior with the Louis Vuitton patterns. The twenty-six-inch floater had Real sitting high and gave him the feeling of power. He now understood the passion that the boys from the South had for big rims.

Pulling into his housing complex, Real thought about how surprised Monique was going to be to see him. She had no idea that he'd been released two months early. He hadn't bothered to tell her because he wanted to see if her reaction to his arrival was authentic.

He and Monique had been together for almost ten years now. They were practically each other's first loves. When Real got locked up, he told her he didn't want her visiting him. He didn't feel like it was right or fair for her to have to go and see him. He especially didn't want her to have to go through metal detectors and uncomfortable body pat downs. Over the couple of years that he was gone, they'd seen each other a few times, but they always made sure to write to each other and talk every week. She was always saying that she would never break their monogamous relationship. He was no fool. He knew that she would eventually do what was only human nature and satisfy her physical urges with someone else. As long as she did it in a respectful way, he could not fault her. In this moment though, he was hoping he wasn't about to come home to her and another man.

Ringing the doorbell, Real turned his back from the window so she could not be able to see his face when she came to the door. After he rang the bell two more times, the door swung open. Standing in the doorway was a little boy about 9 years old. The little boy had on a pair of pajama pants and slippers. He looked up at Real and looked confused.

"What up, little man? Where's Monique?" Real asked as he stepped in the house and looked around. He was still wondering who the kid was.

"Who are you?" The little boy stepped in front of Real before he could take another step.

"Tell her that her boyfriend is here." Looking at the little doorman, Real further wondered who the kid belonged to. He stepped around him and made his way into the living room. It was a very nice apartment. There was an entertainment unit where the television sat. The entertainment unit had an electric fireplace on it and some shelves. On the shelves there were pictures of Monique and some with Monique and her parents. Across from the unit there was a gray sectional with some pillows and a blanket. The whole vibe was warm, inviting, and cozy. Real liked what she'd done with the place.

Heading up the stairs, Real saw that someone was in the shower and walked in through the open bathroom door. Looking at the silhouette in the curtain, he could see the voluptuous outline of Monique. Whether she was fucking or not, he had to put all feelings of doubt aside because even her shadow was fine as hell.

"Auntie Monique! Some guy is here saying he is your boyfriend!" the little doorman yelled out before Real closed the bathroom door in his face.

"Tashawn, I told you if anybody calls, tell them I'm in the shower. You better not open my door for nobody but your father when he finally gets here!" Monique yelled from inside the shower as she turned off the water, not knowing that Tashawn already broke that rule.

Real could feel his nature rise as she pulled back the curtain just enough to reach for a towel hanging on the rack next to the shower. It was now the time to let her know that he was home.

"I see you got a new man in your life."

Real's voice scared the shit out of Monique, causing her to let out a shriek of terror. As she pulled the curtain back slowly to see who was in her bathroom, her shriek of terror immediately transformed into joy. Her towel barely concealed her 36-24-42 frame as she jumped out of the shower into the arms of her lover.

"When . . . How . . . Why didn't you tell me you were coming home, baby?" Monique was so excited that her words were caught up in her throat as her towel dropped to the floor.

"I was tired of being there, so I clicked my heels together three times and said, 'There's no place like home,'" Real joked as he wiped her wet hair from his face.

He could feel the softness of her 36Ds press against his chest as he held her slim waist. Monique was a perfect candidate for *King Magazine*'s centerfold with her flawless caramel skin. She could pose without the need for airbrushing. Her ass seemed to have a mind of its own as it would shake to a rhythm of a beat only it could hear. Many nights that same rhythm would invade Real's dreams, making him thirst for the day they were reunited. Now that the moment had finally arrived, his dreams were about to be reality.

Monique peeked to make sure Tashawn wasn't anywhere in the hallway. She didn't want to risk being seen by her nephew. When she made sure the coast was clear, the two lovers made their way to the bedroom in a matter of seconds. Monique's head damn near hit the wall behind the bed as Real tossed her on the king-size bed and began to take off his clothes. Watching him throw his jersey to the side and begin to take off his shorts, Monique could feel herself getting moist between her legs at the thought of him being inside of her. He was moving too slow for her, so she decided to take control of the action. Sitting up on the edge of the bed with fire in her eyes to match the feelings between her legs, she grabbed him by the waist and pulled him toward her. Almost losing his balance, Real felt his hands being slapped to the side as Monique hastily dropped his shorts and boxers to his ankles and took his manhood in her hand. Before he could get his feet out of his shorts, he could feel the warmth of her tongue run up and down his shaft in slow motion. While cupping his nuts in her hand, Monique continued to massage the head with her tongue as he held her shoulder-length hair between his fingers. Taking him deep into her throat, she was pleased to hear the slight moans of ecstasy escape from his mouth. With one hand between her own legs rapidly rubbing her clitoris with two fingers, Monique's head bobbed back and forth, furiously sucking on Real's dick until she could feel the muscle throb within her cheeks. At the same time, she could feel her vaginal walls contract as she also was about to cum. In another seven seconds, her mouth was filled with four years' worth of built-up passion as Real shot his load down her throat.

Feeling weak at the knees, Real sat down on the bed, still with his shorts and boxers at his ankles, and lay back on the pillow. Without a word, Monique got up and put on her robe and headed for the bedroom. Bewildered at her sudden departure, Real said, "Where are you going? You know a nigga need some time to get back to normal. It's been a long time."

With a sexy grin, she turned around to him and said, "Don't worry, baby. I have a way to energize your rabbit. I'm not letting you get away that easily."

Watching her ass through the robe, Real sat puzzled as she left the room. Taking off his boots, his mind was racing at the thought of what she could have on her mind. Lighting up a Black & Mild cigar, Real lay on the bed awaiting her arrival. Within two minutes, Monique returned with a little pink bag and a glass of ice water. Her grin was still on her face as she strolled in the room.

"What you got there, little lady, a bag of Viagra?" Real joked, still smoking the cigar.

Grabbing his flaccid tool, she looked him in the eyes. "Just my bag of tricks that kept me company while you were away at camp."

Emptying the contents of the bag out on the bed, Monique instructed Real to sit back and relax. Out came a variety of toys: a set of Ben Wa balls, a Super Jackrabbit, a Pocket Rocket, and something that looked as though it could be used to detail a small car, called a Taffy Tickler.

"Before you take another one of those gadgets, you better call 911, because if you're thinking about touching me with one of those motherfuckers, I'm gonna catch another case right now." Real had no idea what was about to go down and was looking for an explanation.

"Boy, this is gonna hurt me a lot more than it's gonna hurt you. Now sit back and shut up. You can either give me what I want, or I'll take it." Still holding his dick in her hand, she was transforming into her dominatrix mode.

Taking off her robe, Monique took a drink of the ice water while taking a cube of ice in her mouth. She then lay down and traced the ice cube across her lips to her chin, then to her neck. With her other hand, she slipped her fingers between her moist pussy lips. She let out a soft moan as she rubbed the ice across her hard nipples, and the more she flicked her clit, the more her temperature rose, causing the ice to melt. Real sat quietly, watching Monique please herself and feeling his manhood stiffen with every moan she let out.

Monique's hand now traced the ice down her stomach past her navel until she reached her sweet spot. For the first time Real noticed a tattoo on her pelvic area. It was a picture of two hearts with a small banner between them that had a caption that read "Real's Love." It seemed as though she was as much of a rider for him as she'd said. As he watched her make the ice disappear in her pussy, he was more than ready to straddle her.

Before he could make a move, she grabbed the Taffy Tickler and turned it on. The low-key buzz at a push of a button brought the toy to life as she brushed the pine-cone-shaped top on her pussy. Her back arched off of the bed in pleasure as she inserted it inside of herself, and regaining her composure, she motioned for Real to take control of the micromachine. Grasping the opportunity to participate, Real grabbed the apparatus by the handle, unknowingly switching the speed control from level one straight to level four. At the sudden acceleration, Monique clutched at the pillow and thrust her hips forward. She was lost in ecstasy as he slowly twisted the machine around in her love box, biting down on her own lip as she held his wrist and trembled, feeling herself about to erupt in delight. Her juices slowly ran out of her to her ass cheeks down to the bed, and it was all that Real could take. He was ready to fuck.

Immediately, Real replaced the Tickler with his tool and began to stroke her intensely. She welcomed him by wrapping her legs around his back, pushing forward, and colliding her pelvis with his. Using his arms to support himself, he exercised his back muscles while penetrating her deep with long, powerful strokes as she clenched his dick with a viselike grip with her pussy, making herself as tight as possible to enjoy every inch of him. The sound of his heavy breathing turned her on more than any of her toys possibly could.

Clenching his teeth, pumping away, he reached under her and grabbed on her firm ass with both hands and squeezed. He could feel her juices flow under her as she climaxed to yet another orgasm, and her fingers dug into his lower back as she pulled him into herself furiously. After another three minutes she began to cum again while cursing and biting Real on the shoulder, demanding that he didn't dare stop. Her pussy walls contracted around his dick while coating it with a thick white liquid, causing a squishing sound. The sound of the headboard banging against the wall echoed throughout the room as Real felt himself about to cum for the second time. Feeling his muscle throb inside of her, Monique knew that he was about to cum and wanted to take him in her mouth one more time. The vein busting out of the side of his neck and his animal-like breathing let her know that he was at the point of an orgasm, so with catlike reflexes, she pushed him off of her and sat up with her mouth open. Like a hose out of control, Real's dick began to spit cum all over. The first stream shot out to her chin and cheek, dripping from her chin to her breasts. Grabbing hold of his dick, she sucked the last bit of cum out of him.

Spent, Real collapsed on the bed sweating and breathing heavy. Looking at his wild sex kitten, he was totally satisfied and could not think about a round three.

"I don't give a fuck if you make that motherfucker spin straw into gold, I gotta take a nap. You got a nigga worn the fuck out." Real lay on his back, trying to catch his breath.

Rubbing his semen on her chest, Monique pet him on his stomach. "Don't worry, baby boy, you can sleep, but when you wake up, please believe that I got some more for you. I'll teach you about going away and leaving me for so long."

"Shit, at this rate you ain't got to worry about that again. Hell, I might get a job at McDonald's just to stay out of trouble." Real smacked Monique on the ass while joking.

"Nigga, you know you full of shit. You'd probably steal the Golden Arches right off of the place," she said, knowing that Real wasn't about to do no shit like that.

"Girl, I'm past the stealing stage of my life. Now I might kidnap that clown Ronald and ransom his ass off for a couple of Big Macs and some fries." Laughing at his own joke, Real lit his cigar again and enjoyed the moment with his baby that he had been dreaming about for so long.

CHAPTER NINE

Feeling the carpet between his toes, Pain walked through his Remington-style home in Hiawassee Oaks. Not much had changed since he had been gone. Kera didn't want to make any changes because everything was a reminder of her man. Entering the bedroom, he could see Kera curled up, sleeping in the same position that he left her in about forty-five minutes ago. It was only five forty-five in the morning. The department of corrections had installed a five o'clock wake-up call in his mind that was hard to readjust from. Realizing there were no more chow halls and count times, he went to the front yard and smoked a blunt while drinking real orange juice. The freedom to do as he wished made the simple things that he once took for granted seem like a luxury.

Opening the door to their walk-in closet, Pain took hold of the pull chain that activated the interior lights. With his wardrobe on the left and Kera's on the right, it seemed like a mini boutique. Most of Kera's clothes still had the tags on them.

She felt no need to dress up in the absence of her man, and he was the only one she wanted to impress. He looked to his left and saw just where he left a gray Rocawear sweatsuit and a pair of retro Jordans. His plans for the day had to start early since they had been postponed for the last forty-eight months.

Now dressed and prepared to hit the street for a trip to the thirty-third precinct, he kissed his woman, who was still curled up in the bed. A smile crept across her face as she opened her eyes to the man she loved. This was a feeling that she long missed but dreamed of constantly whether awake or asleep. To make sure her imagination wasn't taking control of her mind, she reached out and touched him.

"*Buenos dias, papi.*" Kera's accent was a soft spot for Pain, and she knew it.

"Good morning to you too, baby girl. I didn't mean to wake you up until I got back." Pain brushed her hair out of her face with his hands and kissed her again.

"Get back from where? It's still early in the morning. Come back to bed," Kera whined while rubbing her hands on his stomach under his shirt.

"I gotta go and register at the jailhouse or else they'll put a warrant out for me for failure to report and comply." Pain was tempted to crawl back into bed and make love to his woman again, but he knew his first priority was to get to the jailhouse.

"When you get back, I'll have breakfast ready for you. What you want me to make?" Kera asked Pain while heading for the bathroom.

"Anything besides grits and eggs will be fine, but by the time I get back it will be too late for breakfast. Ain't no telling how long I'm gonna be at this shit." Not wanting to go, Pain knew he had to do it.

Surprisingly, Pain was in and out of the county jailhouse within thirty minutes and driving his truck down John Young Parkway. He continued down Colonial Drive, lost in the freedom of being able to move on his own schedule. Now it was time that his schedule involved making some money, and as the thought crossed his mind, he spotted a familiar car riding not too far in front of him. It was a nigga he definitely wanted to holla at because of his hustle in the counterfeit game.

Ox was a nigga who thought about money twenty-five hours a day, eight days a week, and used every resource he had to get it. He first met Pain in Atlanta at the Velvet Room nightclub in the VIP section.

Both had been enjoying the club until some nigga from Decatur thought that he could sell them butterfly ecstasy pills that had the potency *of Children's Tylenol. Pain wasn't a heavy pill popper and neither was Ox, but they knew that within the first twenty minutes of taking the pill they should have felt some kind of buzz. Ox approached Pain first and asked him if it was his imagination or if the pill he took was a bunch of bullshit. Pain agreed that it wasn't having any effect on him. He just took it as a nigga's $20 scam, and he was enjoying the club too much to even stress about it.*

After the club, Pain made his way to his truck in the parking lot, and just when he deactivated the alarm system and opened the door, an unwelcome person emerged from the shadows.

"All right, folk, don't make this harder than it is! Peel off that chunk on your neck and hand me the keys!" The phony pharmacist was now a jack-boy holding a Taurus 9 mm.

Pain stood motionless, looking at the gunman in the face, thinking about his .45-caliber that was right under his driver's seat. There was no opportunity to get to it before the punk could squeeze off a shot. This buster was about to make a quick come-up, and Pain hated the thought of it.

"Partner, you must think this is a motherfucking game! Give it all up or this shit gonna turn from robbery to homicide!" The jack-boy pulled the slide back on the 9 mm and took a step toward Pain.

"You got it, my nigga, ain't no need to shoot. Just take what you want." Pain dropped the keys on the ground and was about to take off his necklace.

About six cars to the left, Ox was sitting in his Lexus SC450, rolling a blunt before leaving the parking lot. When he saw the same nigga who sold him the bogus pill creep up on Pain, he grabbed his .357 Ruger and got down low to make his way to the truck. Even though he didn't know Pain, this punk had conned him out of $20 earlier. Being a con man himself, Ox hated the thought of anybody getting one over on him, whether it be for a dollar or a thousand dollars.

Slowly approaching the robbery in progress, Ox knelt down under Pain's truck and took aim at the pair of Soldier Reebok sneakers. Taking a moment to think, Ox realized that the hand cannon he held would cause too much noise and there would be no way out of the parking area past the police who were posted less than one hundred yards away. Reevaluating the situation, Ox decided to take a different approach. Quietly coming across the truck, he was now only a few feet away from the gunman and Pain.

Coming up from the ground, the jack-boy was now holding the keys to the Suburban with a grin on his face. "Now give up that chunk, fuck-boy. Your punk ass don't need that no more!" Feeling as though he was completely victorious, the gunman was getting cocky with himself.

Pain, still looking at the gun, got a clear view of what he couldn't believe he'd missed earlier. The Taurus was missing the clip! This punk had no bullets. Instantly a sinister grin crept across Pain's face. It was now time to switch the roles up.

"Hey, my nigga, do you know how far the Waffle House is from here? A nigga hungrier than a motherfucker." Out from the shadows, Ox emerged with the nonchalant question.

Making a fatal error, the would-be jack-boy/con man took his eyes off of Pain to see who was talking to them. Before he could focus on Ox, who was standing there brandishing the .357 Ruger, he felt the impact of a powerful right hook that landed on his left temple.

Knocking the assailant to the ground, Pain delivered a kick to the midsection of the bogus gunman with his Timberland boots. Reaching into the car, he retrieved the .45 that was under the seat. The now-dazed thug attempted to get up and run, only to feel the blow across his head by Ox's gun. As the warm flow of blood covered the side of his head, he heard the heavy metallic slide of Pain's gun.

"What da business is now, son! It looks to me like you got something that belongs to me," Pain growled in a low key with his left hand extended while his right hand held the Desert Eagle.

Realizing that his life was now in the balance, the jack-boy attempted to plea, "Folk, you know I was just bullshitting. Ain't no harm, brother. Here. Here goes your keys."

"Cuz, don't forget you owe me twenty dollars for that fake-ass bean you sold me earlier," Ox interrupted while rubbing his temple with his gun.

"Here, bro, take it. My bad. I ain't know that they was fake." The once-robber turned victim pulled out a couple of crumpled-up bills from his pocket along with the keys to Pain's truck.

Confused about who to hand over the stolen property to, the unlucky burglar was frozen in place. Directly in front of him stood Ox with an arsenal that could crack an engine block, and behind him stood Pain with something that looked like RoboCop's sidearm. He put himself in a lose-lose situation that could only lead to his mother crying while wearing a black dress. Tears began to form in his eyes, and his bottom lip began to quiver.

"Stand up, nigga!" Pain barked from behind him, causing him to fumble the keys and money.

"I . . . I'm sorry, bro. Please, I got a little boy at home. Shit has been fucked up for me. I was just trying to make some cash." Through tears and slobber, the little punk was begging for his life.

Stifling a laugh, Ox snatched the money from the boy's hand and counted out $80. "Little nigga, *you mean to tell me that you about to die, and all they gonna find on your body is eighty funk-ass dollars? This shit can't pay for no funeral, stupid-ass nigga!" Ox threw the money back in his face. "Give that man back his motherfucking keys!"*

Taking his keys back, Pain stuck the triangular gun nozzle right in the boy's mouth. "Here's the deal, junior, strip off all your clothes and toss them in the truck!"

Without hesitation, the punk began stripping down until he reached his boxers. As he paused for a second, he felt a kick in the ass delivered from Ox's boot.

"I know you heard the man say strip! We ain't got all day. Now strip!" Ox ordered, wondering what the hell Pain had planned.

Now completely naked with his clothes sitting on Pain's car seat, the boy used his hands to conceal himself. With his face wet with tears and blood, he held his head down in silent prayer, hoping to just be able to make it home.

"By the time I start this truck, your ass better be gone. If not, you will never know what the weather is gonna be like tomorrow!" Deciding to spare the boy, Pain shoved him in the chest with the gun.

"Don't forget your lunch money, little nigga. You just may be able to spend it after all." Ox gestured to the crumpled bills on the ground.

It took about two seconds for the naked boy to streak away from the scene, clutching the money in one hand while covering his crotch with the other.

Since sharing a laugh at a nearby Waffle House after that incident, the two men became friends as well as sometime business partners. Ox would use counterfeit money to lure in dope boys, while Pain used his steel to rob them along with Ox. Little did they know, Pain would break bread with Ox the day after and plot on another dope boy.

While Pain was in prison, Ox kept in touch with him by writing and sending him cash. He was still doing his thing on the street but never forgot his boy. Pain knew that hooking back up with Ox would bring opportunities to get at some major players who may have come up since he had been gone.

Seeing Ox's car pull into the West End shopping mall, Pain pulled in behind him and parked his car.

"It's been a while since I seen that bus on the road. I knew it had to be you, unless Junior decided to go joyriding." After stepping out of his coupe, Ox walked up to the driver's side of the truck and greeted Pain with a pound.

"Yeah, I knew it had to be you in that throwback Lexus. When you gonna upgrade, nigga!" Pain joked with his friend.

"Now, dawg, I was waiting for you to get off vacation so we can get the matching Maybachs." Ox was glad to see his friend home.

Pain and Ox went through the mall talking about old times and times to come. The two ended up in Best Buy so that Ox could purchase a new laptop. He changed laptops as if they were underwear. Whenever he felt his hard drive had too much incriminating evidence of illegal activities, he would replace it after destroying it completely. Pain purchased the new RIM BlackBerry Red to replace his outdated phone, which had been sitting in his drawer for the last four years.

After buying a few items for Kera and Junior, Pain and Ox headed toward the parking lot to get ready to leave. Ox's phone rang, playing the T.I. ringtone "24's." Pain could tell by the expression on Ox's face that it had to do with money.

"It'll take me about two hours to get it over to you. Yeah, we'll do it just like last time. All right, my nigga. Be on time. Peace." Ox's face looked as though he just hit the lottery as he hung up the phone. "I'm glad you off vacation, my nigga. It's time for us to go to work on some cash. Unless they broke your spirit in there," Ox joked with Pain to see where his head was at.

"Willie Lynch couldn't break my spirit. Neither could those soft-ass crackers in them brown uniforms. All they did was make me smarter. Anyway, what's up? You got some work for me?" Pain popped open the trunk and tossed his bags inside.

"These niggas I'm fucking with got a connect and don't know how to use it. They fucking with some *chicos* with major weight, but they copping half a bird at a time. Every time they cop, they mix some of my bills with some authentic money, and the *chicos* don't know the difference." Ox's words were registering in Pain's head quickly.

"So who's the target, these niggas or the *chicos?*" Pain asked, already knowing that he wanted the big dogs.

With a smile, Ox replied, "That depends. Do you want to keep driving that Suburban or are you ready for those matching Maybachs?"

Without a pause, Pain ran his hand across the hood of the truck and said, "Well, big girl, you had your time, but it is time for daddy to move on. I'm gonna miss you."

The two men shared a quick laugh, although they were more than serious about their plans. Knowing that Ox was a die-hard paper chaser, Pain couldn't wait until he got the details of the plans to get at the *chicos*.

Looking at his watch, Ox made plans to meet up with Pain the next day so they could talk more about their come-up.

"These *chicos* are not gonna be a walk in the park. We might need another head or two to make this happen." Ox handed Pain his cell phone number on a business card and gave him a pound.

"I think I got a nigga already lined up. I just got to test the waters first." Pain immediately thought of his old cellmate Real.

"My nigga, make it happen. Holla at me tomorrow morning and let me know what's up." Ox walked across the parking lot and got in his Lexus and drove away.

Starting up his truck, Pain was thinking about whether Real followed through with his plans on getting with that skinny nigga from Tampa. He still had two more days before he was supposed to link up with Real, but by then hopefully they would be able to make their penitentiary promises into a reality.

Reaching over to the Pioneer touchscreen, he cued up his reggae CD and drove out of the parking lot listening to the Sizzla classic "Solid As A Rock."

CHAPTER TEN

"Ain't nothing change, cuzo. The price is still the same. I know Bezo been spoiling y'all niggas while I was gone, but right now I'm taking no shorts. Hell, I'm already showing love. Where else you gonna get a big eight for two stacks?" Fifteen spoke to Kilo while watching the neighborhood addict Rico wash his Cadillac.

"I'm just saying, bro, I got eighteen hundred right now, but I'll straighten you when I get back." Kilo had the other two bills in his pocket but didn't want to come off of it. Just six hours earlier he had to give his girl Shanita $500 for an abortion.

"Look, this conversation is going on too long. Either you got two stacks, or ain't no deal, bottom line. I was doing time while y'all niggas been out there doing fine, and now you want me to look out. This is a grown-man's world, and there ain't no room for crumb snatchers!" Fifteen's words came at Kilo as an insult, and his body language was as though Kilo were just another junkie trying to buy a dime rock with $8 worth of quarters.

Kilo was a neighborhood hustler trying to make his way up, but his habits of trickin' with some ho in the club and snorting powder always brought him back down to square one. The only thing he had to show for his hustle was his dunk that sat on twenty-six-inch rims. Right now, he felt as though Fifteen was trying him like a little boy, and he wanted to prove he was a grown man by slapping the words out of his mouth and the thoughts out of his head with the butt of his 9 mm. The reality of it was that Fifteen was well protected by the chicks monopolizing the state with their product, not to mention his personal goons, Bezo, and some nigga from New York who had shown up a couple of days ago named Real.

Since being on the scene, Real had proved himself as a true soldier with a knockout punch. The Wednesday that Real returned Fifteen's car, they went to a local club in Ybor City called Fuel. After having a couple of drinks and watching the ladies do their thing, the DJ announced the start of the fight night Wednesday competition where the local roughnecks would slug it out for a prize of $500 cash. The prize was nothing compared to the side bets made by the ballers and hustlers who attended the club. Everyone in the club had their favorite fighter who would attend these competitions almost every week, and each time Marco would prove to his opponents that he was the people's champ by knocking them to the canvas. That night Marco was defeated in the third round by Real, who displayed excellent combos to the body and head. Not only did Real leave with the $500, but he also got $10,000 of the $19,000 that Fifteen made off of numerous side bets throughout the club.

Biting his tongue, Kilo listened to Fifteen talk down to him. When he first arrived at the spot he peeped the whole scene out, so he knew his goons were there and probably would jump on him if he so much as raised his voice. The only choice left was to either walk away without the product he came for or reach in his pocket and pay full price. The first option didn't benefit him because if he walked away with nothing, he would have to go to the Haitian boys in Eustis, and they definitely weren't taking any shorts.

"All right, I got you the whole two stacks, but I was hoping to get a little deal. You know shit has been kind of fucked up for me lately. My girl Shanita had to get an abortion and shit, so I had to come out of my pocket with a chunk of change," Kilo explained as he counted out the bills he dug out of the pockets of his shorts that he wore under a pair of Girbaud jeans.

"Shanita!" Fifteen let out a hard laugh listening to Kilo's pathetic story. "That bitch ain't been at no doctor's office unless they give fuckin' abortions at the mall!" Fifteen continued to laugh at Kilo as he took the money out of his hand.

Confused by what Fifteen was saying, Kilo couldn't help but ask, "What the fuck you talking about? Her cousin took her to the doctor's office the other day so she could get that done. She's been crying about it for three days now, talking about how she can't raise no baby by herself!"

"Let me ask you this. Exactly how long have you been a dumbass? Look, I feel kinda bad for you right now, so I'ma keep it real with you. You been chumped, my guy. I don't know what would make you think you can trust that bitch or any bitch out here, but you been getting lied to. Your so-called baby mama ain't use no money for no doctor. What I heard and seen is your girl Shanita been working hard to win my boy over and get him to stay shacked up with her because she like that pipe he been laying down on her. I also do know that the new people's champ just got a new pair of Timberlands and a Rocawear outfit hand delivered by Shanita about forty-five minutes ago." Fifteen waved for Real to come out of the house so he could verify what he just told Kilo.

"What up, my nigga?" Real swaggered up, looking Kilo dead in the eyes. He could feel a lot of heat coming from this kid and was wondering what this was about.

"Champ, this fool said Shanita hit him up for five hundred dollars for an abortion this morning. He thinks Shanita went to the clinic to get it taken care of a few days ago. Tell him what that bitch really got going on," Fifteen said to Real, not giving notice to the anger and embarrassment building up all over Kilo's face.

Real, not really wanting to put his business out there about Shanita and himself, just kept a cautious eye on the hand motions of Kilo. He kept touching his back pocket as though at any moment he might produce a surprise coming from his left hand. Real thought back to that night and was beginning to regret everything he did after the fight.

The fact was that after the club last Wednesday night, he had met up with that girl Shanita. She had gotten introduced to him after his fight. Shanita felt the new people's champ deserved a prize from her. She approached him and found out that he was from New York. She saw how good he could fight and loved the fact that he was fresh out of prison. Shanita had always had a thing for bad boys. She was a real freak when it came to the type of men she preferred. There was something about dick fresh out of prison that she enjoyed. It was like they fucked and came harder than the rest of the men. The only downfall was that they didn't last long at first, but at the same time, they usually were dying to eat some pussy, so either way it was a win-win situation for Shanita. She knew she had to have Real. She wanted to feel him deep inside of her.

After getting introduced, they got to talking, went back to her place, and fucked all night and into the morning. Her phone kept vibrating, and she kept ignoring it. As it reached six in the morning, she finally stepped out to take the call. Real didn't care what she had going on or if she had somebody. She wasn't shit to him. He had his good girl at home. He was ready to head out when she started trying to convince him to stay with her. Since then, she had been trying to lock him down, but Real's mind was on a bigger target, so her efforts wouldn't get her anything more than a mouthful of dick. Real went along with what she was doing. He flirted back, gave her some attention, and convinced her to buy him some gear. Shanita was so eager to get him that she figured she could lie to her other nigga and get him to give her money. Real didn't give a damn what she did. That was none of his business.

"Look here, whatever the fuck y'all niggas got going on, y'all leave me out of it. I damn sure ain't got no time for gossip." Real was aggravated that Fifteen called him over for the bullshit. Since he had been around, Fifteen had done a few things that made him want to just take everything he had then and there. The only thing that made him spare the skinny country boy was Pain. It turned out that the same *chicos* his old cellmate was plotting on were Fifteen's connects. So Real had to play the part for a while longer in order to get the big payoff, but his patience was getting shorter and shorter.

"Nigga, you better do like your boss man says and tell me what the fuck is going on with you and my bitch!" Kilo barked in Real's face with his hand on the grip of the gun in his back pocket.

"Hold on, little nigga. Whatever you got on your chest about some bitch, you better step off and go take it to that bitch, feel me?" Peeping Kilo's stance, Real made one swift motion and pulled out the blue steel .38 Special revolver that he had tucked in the small of his back.

The thought of having to possibly kill this nigga over some pussy didn't sit well with Real, but at the same time he wasn't gonna let some pussy-whipped fool do something to him either. If it were up to him, the situation would not go any further, but it was all up to the nigga Kilo whether somebody would have to take a dirt nap. With the six-inch barrel pointed at Kilo's throat, Real stared into his eyes and saw one thing: fear.

The whole area suddenly got quiet as the two men stood at arm's length. Kilo regretted ever fucking with this girl as he cursed her in his mind. He had no chance to even pull his gun out of his pocket. All he wanted to do was cop some work and go about his business, but his mouth ended up writing a check that his ass couldn't cash.

"My nigga, it ain't the day to die over no pussy. What you need to do is finish handling your business with my man right here and go and check your bitch." Real gave his final ultimatum to Kilo, trying to spare his life

"You dead right, man, you dead right. I don't want no trouble. I just wanted to know what was up with that ho." Kilo gladly jumped on the chance to live another day. He could feel his Adam's apple touch the nozzle of Real's pistol with every syllable he spoke.

"You are smarter than you look, my nigga, so I'm gonna look out for you myself. Instead of that eight that you planned on getting, I'm gonna throw in two more ounces." Real's words made Fifteen's eyebrows rise in shock.

Real took a step closer to Kilo, never lowering his pistol, and reached around to his back pocket, pulling out the chrome Jennings 9 mm that Kilo had concealed. Then he looked over at Fifteen and saw the look of confusion on his face. The two ounces that he promised to Kilo was Real's way of getting back at Fifteen for even provoking this unnecessary confrontation. Real tucked both pistols in his pockets and walked back to the house, leaving the two country boys to finish their business.

"Make sure he gets that!" were Real's final words before he disappeared through the front door.

"You sure he works for you, or do you work for him?" the neighborhood junkie Rico said to Fifteen as he emerged from hiding behind the garbage can, holding the keys to the Cadillac.

Snatching his keys out of Rico's hand, Fifteen headed for the house with intentions of straightening Real out for his act of insubordination. In his left hand he had Kilo's money clutched tightly as he pushed the front door of the house open with the other. No matter how tight he and Real were, he knew that if he let this slide he would feel as though he could do as he wanted, whenever he wanted.

"Check this out. We got to have a talk about who's who around here!" Fifteen said, approaching Real as he was sitting on the couch talking on his cell phone.

Already pissed off by the unnecessary confrontation with Kilo, Real ended his conversation on his phone and looked up at Fifteen. Had he gone on his natural animal instinct, he would have used the two pistols that he had on him to clean out Fifteen's trap house and end all ties here and now. Constantly he had to remind himself that there was a much bigger picture and it was time to get the ball moving. During his incarceration, he spent a lot of time reading books explaining human behavior in order to prepare himself for situations like this. Robert Greene's law number fourteen, "Pose as a friend, work as a spy," was the perfect strategy for right now.

"My nigga, I know this is your show and all, but that nigga had me fire hot for a second. The only reason I spared his ass is because I didn't want to make your spot hot by blazin' his bitch ass right on the front step. Neither one of us need that kind of heat," Real said while pulling some cash out of his pocket.

"That's all well and good, but you giving up my product to that crab don't make no sense to me," Fifteen said while sitting down next to Real.

"That was just to show that there ain't no bad blood between us. These young niggas got to understand that money covers all tracks. That cash will come back five times its worth if you play the little crab nigga right, and besides, I'm gonna pay for them two ounces out of my pocket." Real handed Fifteen a fistful of fifties and twenties that added up to the $1,600 tab.

Fifteen sat back and took in the things that Real was saying and realized that he was making sense. The fact that he was willing to pay for the two ounces made him reconsider his thoughts.

"Cuzo, you know your money ain't no good with me. I tell you what though, that fool still sitting out there and probably pissed on himself. If you want him to have the two ounces, you go out there and serve him yourself. Everything is in the stash spot in the bathroom." Fifteen handed Real back his cash and added, "Remember, this is your play, so I hope you know what you're doing."

"Hey, man, I'm working for the best in the game. Something has got to rub off on me, right?" Real smiled while catering to Fifteen's ego.

It took Real less than ten minutes to retrieve the product from the bathroom and make the transaction with a timid Kilo. He reassured Kilo that the beef between them over Shanita wasn't worth messing up a good business arrangement. Although Kilo agreed, Real knew to keep a cautious eye on this kid for the short period of time he planned on being around. It was time to begin the execution of the plan that he and his cellmate put together and say goodbye to the gun-shaped state of Florida.

"That nigga is about as scared as they get, but that little extra he got sure made his ass happy as fuck." Real swaggered back in the house to see Fifteen smoking on a blunt while looking through his phone.

"Shit, he should be happy. Not only did he get to live another day, but he got blessed with a little extra work. All he gonna do is trick with that same ho. That young nigga ain't got no hustle in him. His main goal is to get by for the day and stunt at the club at night." Closing his phone, Fifteen looked at his watch and knew that his most important task for the day was in only two hours, and he could not afford to be late.

"Check this out. You remember that nigga Pain I was telling you about?" Real asked.

"Yeah, big cuzo from the camp. What's up with him?" Fifteen asked while stuffing some cash inside of an envelope.

"He got a spot out in Mount Dora, and he need to cop some work. I told him that I know some people who could get just about anything that he wants for a good price," Real said to Fifteen as he sealed the envelope.

"Shit, if he way out in Mount Dora, why don't he fuck with the Haitian boys who run shit out there in Lake County? Them cats are strapped." Fifteen began gathering up a few items around the room.

"You know how that nigga is. He'd rather get the most for his cash even if it means traveling all the way to Miami. Besides, why not get money from all corners?" Real's lies rolled out of his mouth with so much conviction that he would even believe it if he were Fifteen.

"All right, I'll see what I can do for him only on the strength that you and he are tight with each other. Right now you, Bezo, and I got to go meet up with Flaco at his spot to handle some shit. You came on the scene at the right time. Soon we really gonna start booming." Grabbing his Cadillac keys, Fifteen headed to the back room to tell Bezo that it was time for them to head out.

"Who is Flaco?" Real asked as he secured the .38 Special in the small of his back, anticipating the worst.

"Cash money, cuzo, cash money. Today is the day that you meet royalty." Fifteen grinned as he put the thick envelope in his waist and headed for the car.

CHAPTER ELEVEN

"Shortie has been in there for a while now. You sure she's all right?" Looking out the window of the rental, Pain's eyes were glued to the entrance of the bank.

"Bro, don't worry about nothing. That paperwork was on point from a brand-new account. Just sit back and chill. She'll be out in a few. I know what I'm doing." Ox took a sip from the Red Bull that was in his hand and leaned back in the driver's seat.

For the last couple of days, Pain had been going around with Ox as he did his daily routines. From eight o'clock in the morning until two o'clock in the afternoon, Ox would send a team of females to different banks to deposit counterfeit checks into accounts that were developed under bogus names. Afterward, they would withdraw a lump sum of the cash when the check was cleared, leaving only enough to keep the account open for more activity. It took seven days for the bank to realize that the checks weren't worth more than a blank piece of paper, and by then Ox's team of angels already would have $10,000 apiece and had moved on to a different city.

Pain had promised Kera that he would one day stop running the streets and would find a legitimate job and give her the security of knowing that her man would not be going back to prison. But now wasn't the time to do it. Last time he had tried turning his life around, he had found a job making doorframes in Umatilla. The job was so bad that not only did it underpay him, but it also left him going home with splinters stuck in his forearms the size of toothpicks. It became clear to him that, no matter what, the 100-hour transition program that was required by the prison was useless. They kept telling them to learn a craft so they could get a good-paying job when they got out, but the truth of the matter was that there was no room in the working world for a convicted felon to make a decent living. The only places that were willing to hire were the lowest of the low. Right now, all Pain wanted was to return to his foundation and build his money back up so he could keep his family in the lifestyle he wanted for them. His plans were to neutralize the operation of the notorious *chicos* and move back to Brooklyn. All he needed was the green light from Real's end.

"See? I told you. There goes li'l mama right there getting in her car. That means Denise and

Carlene should be coming out soon. They know to meet us at the Caribbean Sunshine Bakery on Colonial Drive and John Young Parkway." Ox put the Charger in gear and proceeded out of the parking lot.

"I don't see why you still fuck with this old-ass 1985 scam you got going on. When you gonna upgrade?" Pain knew that Ox had so many ways to make money, but he always went back to the basics.

"As soon as they stop cashing checks in the U.S., then I'll go to Europe, Africa, and Australia. By that time, I'll have enough cash put away to get a cheap Honda space shuttle and go to Mars and do the same fucking thing!" The fact of the matter was that Ox loved the risk of sending someone up in the bank and taking money that didn't belong to them without using force. He always heard of bank robbers giving a teller a note asking for all of the money in their drawer and getting away with it. His bogus checks were the same thing except they gave the exact amount he wanted.

"You ever caught up with your boy from Brooklyn?" Ox asked Pain while merging into the flow of traffic.

"Yeah, he got that nigga Fifteen thinking that I'm ready to cop some weight. Right now he is in good with him, working as hired muscle." Pain couldn't help but laugh at the thought of Real being somebody's bodyguard.

"What up with the rest of the team? The three of us ain't gonna pull this off by ourselves. We need at least one more soldier to make this shit secure." Ox was as eager as Pain to get at the *chicos* but knew that a perfect strategy was a must.

"He'll be at the airport at seven thirty tomorrow morning. I'll be there to pick him up and give him the rundown," Pain answered, thinking about the hell-raiser he sent for.

"Who you got coming? You grinning like you got Hannibal Lecter on the way." Ox laughed at his own joke, but looking over at the expression on Pain's face, he could tell that he just might be close to correct.

"This nigga don't play the radio when it comes to the work! If something needs to be done, please believe this Jamaican nigga is on it. Ain't no bucking the jack when this nigga is at you." Pain knew that he picked the right man for the job.

"Nigga, you telling me that you done had a nigga coming in from Jamaica to get them motherfuckers? You damn sure ain't fucking around with these *chicos*. I like that!" Ox was glad to have Pain back out on the street because he didn't bullshit with getting what he wanted.

"Naw, Reef is up in East Flatbush, Brooklyn, but he is definitely a Jamaican gangster. One of the deadliest I've ever seen." Pain rubbed his hands together just thinking about what was coming up.

The two conspirators pulled into the parking lot of the restaurant and got out of the car. Inside they ordered a little something to eat. Even though they hadn't been doing anything but keeping an eye on Ox's team of angels, they were hungry and ready to stretch their legs. Pain ordered a chicken patty with coco bread with a large cup of peanut punch while Ox ordered a stewed chicken lunch special with some carrot juice. Shortly after they sat at a table, the restaurant door opened and three well-dressed women walked through the door.

"Hey, daddy, did you miss us?" Promise asked, smiling as she gave Ox a kiss on the cheek.

Promise had been on Ox's team for about six years strong. No matter where Ox would travel, she would be ready to ride. Her loyalty to him made her the ride-or-die chick every hustler wanted in their corner. She made sure that all the girls stayed in line and that their money never came up short. On first impression someone would think that she was his wife, especially if they saw her shoulder that had his name tattooed on it.

"Baby girl, you know I missed you. Do you ladies want something to eat?" Ox asked as Promise sat on his lap.

"Naw, I'm straight," Carlene said as she bashfully sat down.

"Shit! A bitch hungrier than a motherfucker. You can sit there acting cute if you want, but I'm gonna order some of this free food. So you better come on." Denise grabbed Carlene by the wrist and led her to the counter.

Promise reached in her Louis Vuitton purse and pulled out three bank envelopes containing $5,500 apiece and handed them to Ox.

"I gave them thirteen hundred apiece instead of fifteen. Them hoes would have been happy with five hundred," Promise said softly in Ox's ear.

"All right, princess, but I want you to take this money and take the girls shopping for the stuff on this list." Ox leaned Promise forward off of his lap and reached in his pocket and handed her a folded piece of paper that Pain wrote some necessities on.

"Two MAC-90s, one Mini-14, three MP5s, two street sweepers. Goddamn, daddy, you guys gonna look for bin Laden or something?" Just like a true wife, Promise wanted to know what her boo was getting into. She knew that although he already had a gun, he kept violent confrontations to a minimum, so this list had to mean something huge was on the way.

"Naw, princess, we going duck hunting, so we need a few toys to bring," Ox joked with her to let the question just fly through the air.

"Well, these ducks must be the size of fucking helicopters with the shit on this list. Oh, wait, you forgot to put in a nuclear bomb! Pain, you better not be trying to get my baby killed with no bullshit!" Promise looked across the table at Pain, who only responded with a smile.

"Shit, if you ain't kill me yet, what makes you think Pain can?" Ox gave Promise a playful yet firm smack on her ass.

"Where we supposed to go get this shit at anyway, Super Walmart?" Promise rubbed the stinging sensation that Ox left on her behind.

"That's the hard part. I need y'all to take a road trip to Georgia," Ox said nonchalantly as though the three-and-a-half-hour drive were around the corner.

"Georgia! You're kidding, right?" Promise knew he was serious by the expression on his face.

"East Point to be exact. There is a store called the Firing Pin, and all they need is identification and a clean record. In the next couple of minutes, you'll be able to buy a nuclear warhead if you want." Reaching back into his pocket, Ox pulled out another knot of money and handed over another $3,500 to make sure all expenses were covered.

"I want you ladies on the road within the next two hours and back by tomorrow morning, understand?" With his final instructions, Ox gave Promise a kiss on the side of her neck and got ready to leave the restaurant.

"Bro, you wanna add anything else to that list before we leave?" Ox asked Pain.

"That's all we need right there. Besides, I ain't gonna give your wife no reason to beat my ass." Pain found the whole scene amusing and wanted to poke fun any chance he had. Ox was always riding him about Kera, so this was a rare time for payback.

"At least Pain realizes that I should be number one. When you gonna see that?" Promise loved the idea of one day being the only woman who would always be there for Ox, but to him it was always business before pleasure. Although she respected that to the fullest, sometimes she wanted him to throw her legs behind her neck and fuck her back loose. Many nights she would masturbate, imagining that her nine-inch dildo was attached to his body.

"Baby girl, you know that you always gonna be my number one lady no matter who comes on the scene," Ox said to pacify Promise so that he could make his exit.

"That's what your mouth says, nigga, but when I come back from this field trip of yours, you better be ready, because I am more than ready!" Promise grabbed at Ox's dick through the Sean John sweatpants he wore. "You lucky that I can't take this motherfucker with me."

"I bet that you would. When you get back, I'll have something waiting for you." Ox broke free of her clutch and gave her another kiss, this time on her lips.

Licking her lips slowly and seductively, Promise softly bit down on her bottom lip, thinking about finally getting what she wanted the most. "You better not be playing with me, boy, or else I just might catch a rape charge."

Walking out of the restaurant, Pain began to tease his boy about what he just witnessed. "I know damn well that the mighty Ox ain't scared of no pussy! What in the hell going on with you? Promise is fine as hell!"

"You fuck her then! I know what I'm doing. She may look good and all, but the bitch is as crazy as they get." Ox sat in the driver's seat of the Charger.

"What you mean by crazy? This chick has been everywhere with you for damn near a lifetime. She can't be that crazy." Pain wanted to know what Ox was talking about.

"Shortie is into that role-play type of shit where she ties niggas up and spanks them and shit like that, and I ain't with it." Ox thought back to the first time he lay down with Promise and she transformed into her dominatrix personality.

"You telling me that shortie done whipped your ass before?" Pain held his stomach, laughing in the passenger seat.

"Naw, but she damn sure told me what she got on her mind. All I could do was tell her that I'll find somebody for her who is into that kind of shit." Ox started the engine and backed out of the parking space.

"Well, when she get back, your ass is in for it. She looked dead serious." Pain cracked the seal on a Dutch Masters cigar and prepared to roll a blunt for the ride.

Forty-five minutes later, Pain sat back and watched the news in his home in Hiawassee Oaks with a glass of straight Hennessy. His eyes were on the screen, but his mind was somewhere else. Suddenly the sound of his house phone brought him back to reality. Usually he would leave the phone for Kera to pick up, but this time he reached for it first.

"Hello." Pain could hear a reggae song playing in the background.

"Wha ya ah sey, boss?" The coarse voice on the other end was unmistakable.

"Reef? What up? What's happening?" Pain didn't expect to hear from him until he was to pick him up from the airport.

"Everyt'ing cris bredren, me deh yah." Over the phone, Reef deeply inhaled as though he was smoking.

"Huh? What you mean?" Pain strained to understand the patois dialect of Reef.

"Florida, mon, we done reach."

"Already! You here already?" Pain sat straight up in his seat with excitement.

"Ya, mon, me and the bwoy Dummy come down fi see da Elephant Man and Movado stage show at da Rotary club. Stone Love a go mash up di place." Reef's words were slow and drawled.

"Where you at now?" Pain was glad to see that his imported killers were there, but he knew Kera was going to trip when she saw them.

"We deh pon di Florida Turnpike now. Dis ya car come in like one blood-clot rocket. Dem Babylon bwoy caan stop us at all. We come in like one Buju lyric. The bwoy Manix sey bring dis down fi ya."

"You remember where I'm at?" Pain wanted to make sure Reef got there so he could catch up on everything.

"Yeh, mon, we soon come breda so you can give us da full one hundred on dem tings you ah talk 'bout."

"All right, son. I'll be here waiting on you." Pain cradled the phone and slapped his hands together in anticipation of the hostile takeover he had planned.

Picking up his BlackBerry, Pain scrolled through the phone list to the final component to his plans: Real. After two rings, the other end was answered, and the sound of club music boomed through the phone.

"What up, dawg?" Real responded, knowing it was Pain.

"We need to talk. When can you get on my side of town?" Pain asked, wondering where his partner was at.

"It's going to be later on tonight, bro. Right now I'm where we both need to be if you know what I mean," Real explained the best he could.

"All right, tonight meet me at the Rotary club. There are some niggas I need you to meet." Pain was about to hang up but then said, "Matter of fact, bring your boy with you."

"You ready?" Real was surprised at Pain's request.

"Naw, bro. We just gonna get better acquainted until the time comes." Pain then hung up the phone and sat back in his living room chair and thought of his next move.

Pain placed another call. "Hey, nigga. I need a couple stacks of that funny money for tonight," Pain said to Ox.

"What's up with tonight? You doing some trickin' or something?" Ox joked on the other end.

"I'm going to meet up with them boys tonight, and I need to make sure I get their full attention," Pain explained as he reached for the blunt in his ashtray.

"You need me to come with you? It would let them niggas know you about business and not bullshit." Ox was more than ready to ride, thinking tonight could be the night.

"Matter of fact we need three cars, so bring out one of your old-schools. Be at my crib at eleven o'clock. Be easy." Hanging up the phone, Pain went to his closet to find something to wear for later on. One thing that was definitely an accessory was his shoulder strap to conceal his trusty Desert Eagle.

CHAPTER TWELVE

Pain and Kera were sitting in the living room watching a movie. It seemed like a chill and relaxing night, but that was far from what was really going on. Junior was supposed to have been home hours ago, but he hadn't called or shown up all evening. It was almost ten o'clock at night, and Kera and Pain had no idea where he was. Last time Kera had spoken with him was this morning. She had confronted him about a phone call she received to notify her that he had missed third period class. She also had gotten on him for failing his art class.

Kera had high hopes that when his father came home from prison, Junior's attitude and behavior would change, but ever since Pain had gotten home, the only thing different was that Junior was actually spending more time out of the house than before. Kera didn't know what to make of how Junior was acting. She thought with Pain being home, Junior would want to spend more time with his father. Whenever they would go to visit him,

Junior would always be so excited to be seeing him. He would even get upset whenever Kera would go by herself and leave him at home. Now that his father was home and they had time to spend together, it seemed Junior was avoiding him like the flu.

"Do you think we should call the police?" Kera said as she pressed to end the call on her phone. She had just tried calling Junior for what felt like the millionth time. At this point his phone wasn't even ringing anymore. Kera figured the phone had probably died. She had been blowing him up between calling, leaving voicemails, and sending texts.

"That will be a waste of time. The police won't do anything because it hasn't even been twenty-four hours," Pain explained to her. He knew better than to go running to the police. They wouldn't care enough to do anything. The second they realized it was a young black boy, they'd most likely put his information at the bottom of the pile and chalk him up as just another at-risk youth running away from his parents' house.

"But he's a minor. That will probably help them speed up the urgency of him missing."

"It doesn't work like that, Kera. I see where you're coming from, but even if they take our information down, they're not going to take it seriously. I'll tell you what though. I'm going to go change and drive around the neighborhood and see if I spot him anywhere. Do you have any of his friends' numbers that you can call to see if he's with any of them?"

"I have a few numbers I can try," Kera responded.

"Okay, that's a start. So I'll go change and you start making some calls," Pain said as he walked off into the room to get on some sweatpants and a hoodie.

Kera went into the kitchen to pour herself a glass of water before heading back to sit on the living room couch. Just as she was about to take a seat, she heard the front door open. It felt like her heart stopped beating as she stood there silently hoping and waiting to see if it was Junior walking through the door. Sure enough, Junior strolled into the house with headphones in his ears as if all was well and without a care in the world.

"Boy, where in the hell have you been?" Kera walked up to Junior and got in his face.

"Seriously, Ma. I'm literally just getting home. I'm not trying to deal with this right now," Junior replied to her.

"Excuse me? Junior, I have been calling you for hours. You are going to tell me where you were and what you've been doing all evening," Kera yelled.

"Look, I've had a long day, and I'm not in the mood to talk. I just want to go to my room and lie down."

"You're not going anywhere until you give me an explanation," Kera said as she stood in front of Junior to block him from moving past her.

"Yo, for real. You're doing the most right now, and you're really starting to get on my nerves."

"Nerves? You got some nerve to walk up in here like this is some sort of revolving door for the homeless. How dare you try to walk past me like I don't do the most for you in this world?" Kera said as she was trying to hold back tears because of how anxious she had been feeling all these hours just holding on to hope while not knowing whether her son was safe.

Junior shot back with an attitude. "Ma, I can't right now. Don't you see I'm dead tired?"

Pain was walking out of the room dressed and ready to hit the streets when he heard Junior snap at Kera. "Whoa, what's up? I know I didn't just hear what I think I heard. Since when is it okay for you to talk to your mother like you talking to some chick in the streets?" Pain interrupted them.

"Man, don't come up in here giving me some lecture like you've been around to raise me. This my house. I've been the man around here while you haven't been here," Junior spat out with disgust in his voice. "I do what I want, how I want, when I want." He rolled his eyes and tried to brush past Pain as if he were some stranger in the streets.

Pain grabbed Junior by the shoulder with a quick swiftness and spun Junior around so fast that he felt whiplash in his neck. Junior did not know that it was possible to turn another person with one hand that hard.

"Who the fuck you think you talking to like that? I'm not one of them bitch-ass niggas in the streets who gonna take that type of disrespect. You got me fucked up in a way that's gonna get you fucked up on the spot talking to me like that!" Pain barked. "Did you forget who the fuck I am, nigga? I'm about this life before I was your daddy, and I'll always be about this life until the day I die. Now that being said, this better be the first and last time you ever think you can come in this house and be disrespectful to me and your mother. If you don't think you can handle that, you can pack your shit and leave up out this bitch!" Pain exclaimed.

Junior and Kera were both startled at this change in attitude from Pain. He'd never spoken to either of them in that tone, which showed them that he did have another side to him they had yet to meet firsthand.

"Did you hear what the fuck I just said?" Pain asked.

Junior was so surprised to hear his father talk to him this way that he didn't know how to respond to his dad. All he felt was his father's large hand gripping his shoulder. "I . . . uh . . ." Junior stammered.

"'I' what, Junior? Use your words and speak up since you so big and bad. 'I' what?" Pain said through his teeth.

Junior was still standing there with his eyes wide open. "I . . . I heard you."

"That's what I thought. Now you're gonna apologize to your mother because your dumb ass must have lost your goddamn mind speaking to her like that. She's the real person who ran this show while I 'haven't been here,'" Pain lectured his son.

With his head down in shame and frustration, Junior managed to mumble out, "Sorry, Ma."

"I don't think a simple apology is going to make up for this one, Junior," Kera replied. "At this point, I don't know what is going on with you. You barely talk to me. When you're home, all you want to do is stay in your room. You used to tell me how much you missed your father. Now he's home and it's like you purposely stay out of the house to avoid him." Kera felt like this was the perfect opportunity to express herself about what she'd been observing as of late.

A silence fell over all three of them. Junior just hung his head low. Pain let go of his son entirely and took a step back.

"Why don't we all go take a seat in the living room?" Pain suggested. Everyone agreed that was the best thing to do at this time. Once everyone had found a comfortable spot to sit in, it was time to have a family conversation.

"Junior, being locked up taught me a few things that helped me grow from an immature person to the man I'm still growing to be today. You have to understand that we have to look out for each other in this house. I need to know, where have you been this evening?" Pain asked his son.

"I was at the library," Junior admitted. "I went there after school because I like to sit by myself and listen to music on my headphones while I draw."

"And why couldn't you call and tell me that?" Kera asked him in an accusing way.

"Because then you would've told me I should come home and eat and that I can listen to music here at the house," Junior responded.

"Okay, and what's wrong with that?" Kera wasn't sure why she felt like she was being accused of something, but in a way she felt like she needed to defend herself.

"Forget it. You don't understand." Junior sounded frustrated. He turned toward Pain. "Look, Dad, I'm sorry I came off disrespectful. It's been a lot for me to adjust to with you coming home and stuff. I'm working on it." He really meant what he said.

"I get that you're going through changes and adjusting to things, but I'm going to need you to mind yourself. Don't forget your place in this house. You are still the child, and we are the adults."

"Okay. I understand. I've had a very long day. Can I just go to my room and be done with things for tonight?" Junior asked. He was praying to God that they'd just let him go to his room.

"All right. You can go."

"Thank you." Junior sounded relieved to hear them say he could leave to go to his room. He bolted straight down the hall and closed the door behind him.

Kera and Pain just sat there looking at one another.

"What in the hell just happened?" Kera looked at Pain with a bewildered look on her face. "It's like I'm living in the matrix lately. Nothing he does makes any sense to me." She leaned in and was speaking so low she was almost whispering. She didn't want Junior to hear what she was saying.

"Yeah, that was unexpected. You told me he'd been acting up, but this was far from what I expected, especially at this age. I know boys want to flex their way through the teen-to-man changes, but usually it doesn't happen until later." Pain had to admit he wasn't fully prepared to handle his son's new big-boy attitude. Ready or not though, Pain was his father, and he wasn't going anywhere this time. Pain made a mental note to make sure he had more one-on-one conversations with Junior so that they could start bonding on a deeper level.

"Don't worry, babe. I'm going to talk to him more and see where his head is at. He's a good kid deep down. It's hard being a minority male in society right now. I'm going to give him some space for now, but I promise I'm going to speak to him, and things will change for the better around here. Daddy's home, baby. I got us!" Pain said as he leaned in to give Kera a kiss.

"Love you, boo," Kera said after their third little peck on the lips. Kera couldn't put into words how much she loved that man. She prayed to God that she would never lose him again. She couldn't even fathom what she would do if something were to happen and he had to go back to prison for another bid. Kera shook her head and tried to clear her mind of the negative thoughts that were starting to creep in. *Things are going to be just fine.*

CHAPTER THIRTEEN

"What time your boy gonna get here, cuzo? We been here for almost an hour now." Sipping on his Rémy Martin, Fifteen looked at his watch.

"He's parking his ride now. He just hit me on my phone to make sure we was here," Real answered while licking the blunt of purple haze that he just rolled.

"This shit is packed, these dreads are thick up in here, and the babies are throwing they asses everywhere. I know I can find me a new baby mama up in here." Fifteen was enjoying the atmosphere of the Rotary club even though it wasn't really his type of crowd.

It took a lot of convincing for Real to get Fifteen to come way out to Orlando to a reggae club. Bezo was standing close to his boss man like a trained Rottweiler to make sure nothing would go wrong. Real made a mental note to make sure Bezo wouldn't get in the way when it was time to handle his business. Since he came on the scene, Real could feel slight tension from Bezo and knew that eventually he would have to get him out of the way by any means necessary.

"Ay yo, Beez, you ain't gonna babysit that Heineken all night, are you?" Real teased the big man to break the ice.

"I'm straight, folk. I like to stay focused at all times. You never know what can pop off. Plus, we are here for business, right?" Bezo said while scanning the room as though he were a Secret Service agent guarding the president of the United States.

"It's all right, cuzo, we here to chill tonight. Ain't no nigga in here thinking about nothing but these hoes." Fifteen was hypnotized by a girl wearing a miniskirt whose ass was bouncing to the tempo of the reggae music booming out of the speakers surrounding the club.

"Well, I'm gonna get me another drink. Y'all niggas straight?" Real turned around to get the bartender's attention over the crowd of females parked at the bar trying to get their free drinks before twelve o'clock.

"What's happening, champ?" a voice came from over Real's shoulder. Turning around quickly, he saw his ex-cellmate standing there with another guy he had never seen before. "You gonna give your boy a shot at the title or what?"

"What up, my nigga? I was starting to think that wifey put you on a curfew and you couldn't come out to play," Real joked as he gave Pain a dap with a shoulder hug.

"Naw, dawg. It took forever for us to get here from out in Mount Dora 'cause the police was spot-checking cars on the 441," Pain lied to play his role to the fullest, realizing that Fifteen was only a few feet away. "Anyway, this is my man Ox. We in this thing together, so where I go, he goes."

"I feel you, son." Reading between the lines, Real fully understood the part Pain was playing. Reaching out with his right hand, he gave Ox a pound. "What up, son? Chillin'?"

"Everything good, son," Ox replied. He already heard about Real, but this was the first time they were officially meeting. Compared to the two Jamaicans who played incognito in the crowd, Real was the only nigga besides Pain he wouldn't mind working with. Both of the Jamaicans gave him the creeps, especially Dummy.

Not too far in the crowd, Pain's imported assassins stayed low-key blending in with the dark areas of the place. A cloud of weed smoke seemed to linger over them as they both puffed on separate spliffs, and no matter how much they smoked they were always on point. Reef stood at five feet eleven but had the heart of a lion and didn't fuck around when it came to making anyone respect him and his lifetime friend Dummy. He was a brown-skinned brother with dreadlocks that reached to the center of his back. He kept them tied up in one bundle with an ice, gold, and green bandana.

His most distinguishing feature was a scar on his face that started at his ear and traveled to his chin. The only person who knew how the scar got there died minutes after he put it there. The three-star ratchet that made the permanent mark on his face was now in his back pocket wherever he went.

Dummy was a stocky man who was only five foot seven but put fear in the heart of many who saw him. He was a darker brown than Reef, with shoulder-length dreadlocks with brown tips that he let hang in his face, which gave him a more sinister look. Looking into his bloodshot hazel eyes, you would never see remorse for all the killing he had done. Around his throat was a childhood scar from a thick rope that his stepfather left while attempting to hang the child from a tree. If it hadn't been for his mother chopping his drunken stepfather in the neck with a machete, the boy would have been doomed. Tragically the young boy's vocal cords were severely damaged and left him without the ability to speak. Since that moment in his life, the mute Jamaican had been not only physically scarred but also mentally transformed into a heartless individual with no appreciation for life.

Watching from the crowd, the two Jamaicans could see Pain and Ox talking to the man they said was a part of their operation. At the same time, they noticed two other men who stood only a few steps away watching Pain's every move. The bigger one of the two seemed to have a chip on his shoulder as he watched Pain. This didn't sit well with Reef, so he motioned for Dummy to get closer to the men. With stealth movements, Dummy found himself only two feet away from the mystery men and waited on Reef's signal.

"You remember Fifteen, don't you?" Real motioned toward Fifteen with his head so that Pain could see.

"Yeah, I remember son from the camp we just left. What's up with you, homie?" Pain gave Fifteen some dap. Seeing Dummy appear from what seemed to be out of nowhere, he could only silently pray that Fifteen didn't make any wrong moves. It was much too early in the game for Dummy to shake things up.

"What's happenin', cuzo? Looks like the free world treating you good," Fifteen responded, adding a shoulder hug.

"Shit is only as good as you make it, dawg, and every day is a hustle, feel me?" Pain only hoped that Reef had control over his sidekick. "I see that you are taking good care of my boy. That's mad love, son."

"Now that we all face-to-face, we can talk about some real shit. I think I found you a decent connect for what you want," Real said, interrupting the phony reunion.

"I knew I could depend on you, homie. Who is it, and what price is they talking about?" Pain was happy that Real got straight to the point.

"My man right here can get you just what you want, and I guarantee that the price would definitely lock you in." Real placed his hand on Fifteen's shoulder to indicate that he was the man to talk to.

"Yeah, cuzo, the champ here has been telling me that you got a setup out there in Mount Dora. Since you and him is tight, I'll work with you as long as we both benefit." Fifteen looked Pain right in his eyes to let him know he was really about his business.

"Money is always right on my end, so all we can do is benefit." Pain felt a little irritated at Fifteen's statement but kept his composure. He knew that he had to get the skinny nigga's attention by giving him an opportunity at some big money.

"Let's start with the basics first before I make anything official. What are you trying to get?" Fifteen put his empty glass on the bar, waiting to see where Pain's head was at.

"Can you fill an order for twenty birds? If not, we really ain't got to talk no more."

Pain's request hit the Tampa boy's ear harder than the heavy bass line that was shaking the club. "As long as the money's right, cuzo, I can get you Escobar's daughter." Fifteen's attempt at humor was only funny to himself.

"That ain't what I asked for, playa. Just tell me what price you got for me, and if it's showing me the love that my dawg has been promoting, then we can write this shit in stone." Pain locked eyes right back with Fifteen to let him know that he, too, was about business.

"You talking about two hundred and fifty stacks flat as long as I ain't got to transport it." After some quick math, Fifteen came up with that figure and waited to see if Real's boy was here just to talk or if he was serious. "With that kind of love, we might as well get married."

"All right then, homeboy, it looks like Real came through big time for me on this one. I'm gonna holla at you tomorrow by noon for the spot to meet up with you at. I hope you like small bills because that's what I'm coming with." Pain shook the Tampa boy's hand, and for the first time, he took notice of the stare that Bezo had on him.

"You all right, son? You know me from somewhere or something?" Pain stepped toward the big man, only to be stopped by Real.

"That's just Bezo, son. He work with us. That nigga just uptight all the time, always on the job. All work and no play will make Bezo an unhappy boy." Real tried to bring light to the situation with humor.

"Ain't no time for playing. I don't get paid for playing this shit. Ain't the NBA," Bezo said with aggression, attempting to leave the impression that he wasn't to be fucked with.

"Cuzo, I thought I told you before that tonight we just chillin'. The nigga is here for all the right reasons, so just chill and don't lose your head." Fifteen didn't want his watchdog to run off the money before it started to come.

Within earshot, Dummy had his hand on the grip of the Beretta that he had concealed under his Bathing Ape shirt. He was more than willing to fill Bezo's spine with the hollow points that laced the clip. Without a thought, the silencer-equipped gun was discreetly aimed at Bezo's back, and a small red dot danced on his spine. As his thumb slowly cocked back the hammer and the thrill of a kill rushed through his body, he felt a touch on his shoulder that could only belong to one person.

"Just cool, breda, everything criss. Come mek we go beat two Guinness inna deh nite yah." The voice of his partner Reef crept in his ear.

Without hesitation, Dummy tucked the gun back under his shirt and followed his partner to the other side of the bar and purchased the two stouts. Reef knew what his partner was capable of, but right now wasn't the time. Bezo's attitude bought him the number one spot on the list of those who had to go. It was just a matter of time.

When the club was coming to closing time, the parking lot was thick with everyone making plans for an afterparty or just a late-night rendezvous. Ox got the valet to bring around his car while Pain and Fifteen made arrangements to get together later that day for the start of their business. Bezo pulled up in Fifteen's Cadillac and threw up the butterfly doors to let the driver get in.

Putting the car in park, the valet walked around and handed Ox the keys. Although a native New Yorker, Ox also had a love for old-school cars. At Pain's request, he brought out one of his favorites: his '59 Chevrolet Impala hard-top convertible. The gypsy red paint with all original chrome pieces and ornaments were complemented by the white trunk. Ox didn't want to ruin the car's value by following trends and putting big rims on the car, so he kept it low with some chrome thirteen-by-seven Daytons wrapped in whitewall Vogue tires. From the looks at the body, Fifteen was impressed along with many others in the parking lot.

"Y'all boys ridin' decent, cuzo. That's you?" Fifteen said as he walked around the car.

"Yeah, man, a little something a nigga put time into," Ox humbly replied as he pushed the automatic starter on his key chain to bring the car to life.

"What you got under the hood?" Fifteen was fascinated with the car.

"She's running on an eighty-six GMC three fifty small block with a lead block carburetor and accessories." Ox felt as though Fifteen was testing him. With another push of a button, he let down the top, exposing the interior. The red and white vinyl specifications blended perfectly with the red carpeting, making the car look like it was straight off the showroom floor.

"Goddamn, cuzo, I know some cats who would pay a grip for the ride. You trying to sell it?" Fifteen inquired as he spotted the chrome shift knob and custom chain steering wheel.

"Naw, my nigga, she ain't for sale. I put too much heart into this one right here. I tell you what, I got a seventy-two GTO at one of my spots in Tennessee I'm working on that you can finish, and I'll give you a good price," Ox lied just for the hell of it.

"We might work something out, cuzo. I can do some things with that motherfucker. This year I'm trying to crush the classic reunion," Fifteen said as he headed for his car. "I'll holla at you later."

As Pain and Ox got into the Impala, they spotted the rented Charger with the two Jamaicans pulling out of the parking lot and going toward the gas station across the street.

"Tennessee?" Pain asked, looking at Ox.

"Mount Dora?" Ox asked while putting the car into gear.

"Why is it that all the bustas got all the shit that a real nigga can't get his hands on? This little nigga don't deserve to be able to serve an ounce, much less be able to serve twenty birds." Ox sounded disgusted as he saw Fifteen was still watching his ride.

Activating the old-school two-pump, three-battery hydraulic setup in the trunk, he dropped the car down low and began to creep out of the parking lot, illuminating the ground with a red Yankees emblem courtesy of the under-car light kit.

"That's where we come in at, homie. Don't worry about nothing. By the time we through with him, he'll be lucky to have a hand to wipe his ass with." Pain picked up his phone and dialed a number.

"What about that other nigga he with?" Ox asked, referring to Bezo.

"You mean that nigga he used to be with. I'm gonna take care of that right now."

Pain spoke into the phone, giving some brief instructions.

"What about your boys from up top? We gonna link up with them tonight or what?" Ox asked while turning on the Kenwood head unit.

"Naw, son, them boys are going to scratch that itchy-ass nigga. We don't need any obstacles at all." Pain lit the blunt that was resting in the ashtray.

The sounds of Jay-Z's "Blue Magic" boomed out of the Flame Series subwoofers from the back seat of the Impala.

CHAPTER FOURTEEN

Within an hour and fifteen minutes, the Cadillac pulled into the driveway on Hillsborough and Fifteenth Street. The day went by smoothly. First there was the meeting with Flaco at his strip club to make sure that their biggest shipment of cocaine was here. With the price Flaco wanted for it, there was nothing but the chance to profit. The beauty of it all was that it was all quick access, no waiting for a new shipment. If this nigga Pain was about what he said he was, Fifteen would be able to move the works as quickly as possible. Getting out of the car, the trio got prepared to go their separate ways until later on.

"Bezo, I want you here by two o'clock so we can get this shit together," Fifteen ordered his number one watchdog. "This time it's about work, so I need you on time and on point."

"I am always on time, if not early. This shit ain't never been a game to me," Bezo said, walking toward his Monte Carlo.

"Champ, I need you here about three. By that time we will be already set up for the deal with your man." Fifteen wasn't ready to show Real his major stash house just yet. Although he liked Real, he still had to wait to see how his first major play went down.

"Aye, aye, Captain. I'll be here. Right now I'm heading to the crib to get some sleep." Real started up his Acura and threw up a deuce sign before peeling off.

"You sure these niggas got the money straight for this shit?" Bezo leaned out the window of his Monte Carlo while watching Real's taillights disappear down the road.

"Well, cuzo, we damn sure gonna find out later. If these niggas come with some bullshit, I'll let you handle them however you want," Fifteen said as he lit up a cigarette.

"What about your so-called people's champ?" Bezo asked.

"Me and the nigga is straight, but you know what they say. MOB: money over bullshit!" Fifteen took a pull on his cigarette.

"I'm glad to see that you ain't getting soft over the New York clown." Bezo put his car in gear and pulled out of the driveway to head to his apartment.

Fifteen watched his boy ride out and then extinguished his cigarette on the ground before walking in the house. One block away, a smoke-filled Charger came to life and followed the Monte Carlo. The all-black car had been sitting patiently, waiting for the right time, and during that time the occupants decided to make it all worth the wait.

A mile and a half out from Fifteen's house, Bezo pulled into his housing complex, talking to his baby mother on the phone. If he hadn't been trying to get some late-night company from her, he might have noticed the unexpected guests not too far behind him.

"You got your sister there, so just bring your ass on," Bezo said into the cell phone as he opened his apartment door. "All right then, hurry up and come through." As he stepped in the apartment, he closed his phone and instantly felt an impact to the back of his head.

Falling to the ground, Bezo fought to stay conscious only to feel his gun being removed from his waist. He couldn't think of who it could be. Finally he looked up and saw two complete strangers, and instantly he realized it was a robbery.

"You motherfuckers take what you want and get the fuck out of here, but I swear you'll never enjoy that shit." Bezo tried to be as much of a man as possible.

"Pussy hole, you really tink sey ah thief we come fi tief from you? Naw, man, a bigga tings a gwan," Reef said as he rested the cricket bat on his shoulder.

"What the fuck y'all niggas want?" Bezo lay on his back, covering his face and hoping not to get another hit from the thick bat. From behind Reef, Bezo could see a second man emerging with a long machete in his hand.

"Mi friend here no like you 'cause you favor him daddy. Since him daddy nu deh yah him a go git your rass same way." Reef stepped over Bezo and walked farther into the apartment, dropping the cricket bat and pulling out his Walter 9 mm equipped with a silencer.

Sweating and looking at the cold stare of Dummy, Bezo was trying to think of a way to survive these two psychos who had him captive in his own home. "Ay, man, I got about eighty grand. Y'all can take it! Just don't kill me, man, please!" Bezo pleaded.

"Yo hear the bwoy, Dummy, him sey take it and don't kill him, please." Reef laughed at the big man's begging.

"Come on, folk. I got a little girl. Please," Bezo begged while being penetrated by the demonic stare of Dummy.

"Mi tell you what, show mi de money, an' if Mr. Dummy here sey everyt'ing criss, mi let yu live," Reef said while kneeling over Bezo with the gun pointed in his eye.

"It's right in the bathroom, folk. I'll show you." Bezo attempted to get up only to get slapped in the face with the side of the machete.

"Dummy sey you fi crawl pony u belly an mek haste," Reef said with a laugh, watching Bezo hold the side of his face in agony.

Following instructions, Bezo crawled on his stomach to the bathroom with the two intruders walking with him step by step. With the back of his head throbbing and bleeding along with his face, which was on fire from the lash of the flat side of the machete, he prayed to survive so he'd get a chance to get his revenge when they left. Who these men were and why they chased him to fuck with him was still a mystery to him. It didn't matter though because when the tables turned, their asses were as good as dead.

"Mi nuh si no money yet, big man, ah ramp you ah. Ramp wit we or what." Reef took aim at the back of Bezo's head.

"It's right here. I ain't shitting you, man." Bezo reached for the back of the toilet. He got a hard kick to the back of the head, causing his face to crash into the porcelain bowl.

"Mi friend nu trust you fi some reason. So you betta nuh move or else mi nuh response fi wha him do." Reef reached for the back of the tank and grabbed a plastic bag duct-taped to it that contained some thick stacks of money in rubber bands.

"I told you. Now pleaaase just take it. I ain't going to say shit to nobody!" Bezo pleaded through a mouthful of blood.

"Hold on, my yout. Before we lef ya, tek off dat de chain and rest it in a mi hand." Reef extended his left hand. The gun in his other was aimed at Bezo's face.

"Here. Here you go. We straight now, right?" Trembling, Bezo was willing to do whatever it took to get rid of the intruders.

"Well, breda, wha you tink? De big man did come through wid de money. You ready fi lef ya or wha?" Reef asked Dummy, already knowing the answer.

With one swift swing, Dummy brought the machete down on the back of Bezo's neck, almost cutting straight through. In agony and shock, Bezo let out a shrill cry as Dummy took another swing and completely decapitated the man. A thick stream of blood shot on the wall of the bathroom and on Reef's shirt as Bezo's head fell to the ground with its eyes still open, facing his own body.

"Hey, bwoy, watch wa you ah do. You no si mi have on mi good shirt!" Reef yelled at Dummy, who was picking up Bezo's head off the ground. With a wicked smile, Dummy took a toothbrush off the sink and gouged Bezo's eyes out of their sockets before flushing them down the toilet. Dummy propped the head on top of the tank of the toilet and walked calmly out of the room.

"Hey, madman, you know se you a go pay fig it mi shirt cleaned." Walking behind Dummy, Reef continued to playfully chastise his friend. Under his arm he carried the plastic bag that had Bezo's contribution to their cause.

As they opened the door to leave, they were greeted by a young lady who was about to knock on the door. Since Bezo had claimed to be alone for the night, seeing the two Jamaicans, she silently cursed, thinking that he was about to pick up and leave to hang out with his hoodlum friends.

"Wha gwan, miss pretty girl?" Reef said as he stepped past Bezo's baby mother with Dummy following close behind.

"Hi. Is Bezo about to leave or something?" she asked with a slight attitude.

"Na, mam, him in a de bathroom. Him no feel too hot right now him ah try fi get him head straight," Reef said on his way to the car while the woman walked in the house.

Before the two reached the car, Dummy turned around to reenter the apartment.

"Cha, man, we nuh have all night fi play," Reef said as Dummy kicked in the door of Bezo's apartment.

The night was silent for another five minutes, and then Dummy returned to the Charger and sat in the passenger seat in comfort. Reef knew that Dummy was an efficient killer who never left any loose ends.

"So wha gwan wild de girl? She see her man?" Reef asked, putting the car in gear.

From his front pocket, Dummy produced two objects that would have made anyone gag. Reef looked over at his friend and jumped back at the mute man's package. In his hand he held the pretty brown eyes of Bezo's girlfriend.

CHAPTER FIFTEEN

At five minutes to three o'clock, Real pulled up to Fifteen's house to find him pacing back and forth with his phone in his hand. The look of frustration was imprinted on the Tampa boy's face as he talked loudly into the phone. Real only assumed that it was somebody who was short on their money, or maybe there was a complication with the *chicos*.

"You need to get on point and get over here! You know we got shit to do, and we already behind schedule by an hour!" Closing his phone, Fifteen looked at his watch and cursed loudly. "Fuck!"

"What up, my nigga?"

"Bezo is probably laid up with some bitch somewhere and ain't answering his phone. That's the hundredth message I done left on his phone." Fifteen pulled a Newport out of his pack and reached in his pocket for a light.

"Shit, I ain't know that uptight nigga even got pussy," Real laughed, trying to lighten up the vibe.

"This ain't no time for jokes. Bezo knows we got shit to handle. Him fucking up makes me look like a fuck-up, and that fucks up my money. I don't care if he's with Janet Jackson. He better roll off that ho and come handle this shit!" Fifteen was so mad that he spat as the words came out of his mouth.

"Why don't you just go to the nigga's crib and see what's up?" Real asked as his own cell phone vibrated in his pocket.

"A nigga ain't got to come wake me up when it's time to handle business. That's what's wrong with these niggas running around calling themselves hustlers nowadays. They ain't got their fucking priorities straight!" Fifteen opened up his phone to call Bezo again.

"Holla at your boy!" Real answered his phone. "What up, dawg?"

"Just chillin', homie. Where you at?" Pain asked on the other end. He was counting the counterfeits that had been manufactured.

"I'm out here in Tampa waiting for this nigga to show up. Why, what's the deal?" Walking off the porch, Real saw that Fifteen was leaving another message on the phone.

"Tell your boy that everything is ready on my end. I'll be heading out to that address in about another hour." Sitting in Ox's house, Pain closed a knapsack full of money and picked up one of the guns that Promise brought back from Georgia.

"I'm going to tell him, but he waiting for that nigga Bezo to show up so he can get the shit you asked for. Right now he tripping because the nigga ain't answering his phone," Real said quietly into the phone so that Fifteen could not hear.

Pain gave Real the brief rundown on why Bezo would not be showing up anytime soon. Real kept his composure on the phone so that Fifteen would be clueless of who he was talking to or what he was talking about. He was glad to know that Bezo was permanently out of the picture. Without him, Fifteen's weak operation was even weaker, which gave them greater advantage. He only wished that he could have seen the fuck-boy's face as he met his demise. Before hanging up the phone, he told Pain to call Fifteen himself and confirm their prior arrangements.

"Who that was, cuzo?" Fifteen said with frustration as Real got off the phone. "Was it that nigga Bezo?"

"You know that nigga don't call my phone. That was that bitch Shanita trying to get a nigga to come over so she can suck me up," Real lied with a straight face.

"Y'all niggas is a trip! Y'all more focused on these hoes when there is money to get. Next thing you going to tell me you about to go fuck this bitch!" Fifteen threw his hands up in the air, thinking that he was not going to able to get his shit together in time.

"Hold on. First of all, I ain't that nigga. I'm where I'm supposed to be. I'm on time, and I ain't said shit about leaving to go nowhere because, as far as I'm concerned, one monkey don't stop no show. You said that you ran shit around here, so why the fuck you waiting on this nigga? If he don't want no money, fuck him!" Real's quick speech brought Fifteen to the realization that, with or without Bezo, he had shit to do.

Just then Fifteen's phone rang. Thinking that it was Bezo, he looked at the caller ID on the display screen. Seeing an unfamiliar number on the screen, he answered, not knowing who to expect on the other end. The brief conversation he had on the phone made up his mind that there was no more time to wait for Bezo. There was money to be made. Hanging up the phone, he walked to the passenger seat of Real's Acura and opened the door to get in.

"That must be that nigga finally waking up. What that motherfucker had to say for himself?" Real asked, knowing damn well that it wasn't anybody but Pain.

"Naw, cuzo, that was your boy from last night. He got his shit together, so it's time we get our shit straight," Fifteen said as he sat back in the passenger seat.

"So what we doing now?" Real started the engine without any idea where they were going.

"Well, cuzo, it looks like you just graduated to the head of the class. We got to go back to Flaco's spot and get this work. I hope you got some space in the trunk." Fifteen pulled another cigarette out of his pack and lit it.

"That's what I'm talkin' about. Let's get this cash. After this shit go down, I'll personally buy your boy a watch so he can be on time from now on," Real joked as he bent the corner in the Acura.

Back at Ox's house in Sanford, Pain sat back, wearing a pair of plastic gloves, checking the guns Promise brought. He wasn't in the bedroom. Ox was paying his dues to Promise for her delivery of the small arsenal.

Dummy and Reef were on their way to the house from their hotel on International Boulevard. Pain let them drive the Skyline that they brought down from New York so they would be guaranteed to be where they needed to be on time. After Reef told him the details of what happened at Bezo's house, he knew that this lick was as good as money in the bank. The sixty grand that they gave him also was a sign of true loyalty. In the back of his mind, he could only hope that Real could keep Fifteen on a short leash so that everything would be accessible.

"All right. Cuzo, pull into the parking lot right next to that Lincoln over there," Fifteen said, directing Real to park next to Flaco's spot.

"Damn, whose car is that? That shit is clean as a motherfucker!" Real said as he pulled next to the '63 Continental convertible.

"That's Flaco's ride. He loves the shit out of it, too, so don't let your door hit that motherfucker. That mint green paint is easy as fuck to show a scratch." Fifteen got out of the Acura and headed for the club entrance with Real next to him.

Inside the club, there were only a few patrons because of the early afternoon hour, yet the girls on the poles were working hard for their tips. One girl was in the back corner with a customer, giving him a buck-naked lap dance. The harder she ground on his dick, the more money he pulled out of his shirt pocket and placed in her hand. The place was clean with an aroma of body sprays and wet pussy lingering in the air. The DJ was playing Flo Rider's "Low" while the dancers ground on the poles to get the attention of the few customers.

"You *vatos* are late. I thought you were better than that, homes." From the back table, Flaco walked up to Fifteen, looking at his watch.

"My bad, Flaco. I would have been here, but—"

"'But'? Did you say 'but'? Look around you, homes. There are plenty of butts dancing around here. The last thing I need is another butt. What I need is for you to be on time!" the five-foot-three

Mexican chastised Fifteen like a child, not allowing him to tell him his sad story.

"You right, Flaco. It won't happen again. I'm here now to pick up what we talked about," Fifteen said, hoping that Flaco wasn't about to give him a lecture on responsibilities. Bezo was definitely going to get his ass chewed out for what he caused.

"Oh, now you want to get to work, eh? You sure that no more 'buts' will happen, especially with the dinero?" Flaco asked, walking toward the back of the club.

Keeping quiet so that no further chastisement would come, Fifteen and Real followed Flaco to the dancers' dressing room. Flaco told the three girls who sat in the front of a small plate of cocaine to get out of the room, and he locked the door behind them. After securing the door, Flaco went up to what appeared to be a fuse box and flipped two switches, causing one of the wall mirrors to slide open to reveal a secret room. The three men stepped into the dark room. This was Real's first time in Flaco's hideaway spot, so he didn't know what to expect.

Flaco pulled the light's chain, and the entire room was illuminated. To Real's surprise, what he saw was a big payoff for all the time he spent being friendly with Fifteen. There was more cocaine than he ever could have imagined, and in the corner was a table that seemed to have more money on it than inside a Brinks truck. It became crystal clear that, for this roomful of treasure, a couple of people would have to die. Luckily his team was a lot more prepared to kill than this little Mexican and this skinny nigga from Tampa were. At least, that was what he thought.

CHAPTER SIXTEEN

"I can't complain at all, homie. A lot of niggas claimed to be able to deliver, but you came through. Even though I been out here for twenty minutes, it was worth the wait and traveling time," Pain said while examining the contents in the trunk of the Acura.

"You know what they say, cuzo. Good things come to those who wait," Fifteen said with a grin as he closed the knapsack that was filled with Ox's best counterfeit work.

"We got a car on the way to carry this shit back to Lake County. The girls should be here in about five minutes." Pain closed the trunk and pulled a Black & Mild out of his pocket and lit it. "Ox, call baby girl to make sure we don't be out here all day."

"There goes our ride turning the corner. Anybody want some ice cream?" Ox gave a nod toward an oncoming vehicle that was one of his other little makeover projects that he never finished.

Fifteen was the first to look down the block. The only car he saw was an ice cream truck slowly making its way toward them. Ox stepped out to the sidewalk with a few dollars in his hand to wave down the truck. The truck came to a stop right at the end of Fifteen's driveway as Ox approached the custom-made Chevy Express's side window. The ice cream decals camouflaged the white van that was running on a 350 small block with a deep freezer on the inside that had Popsicles, ice cream sandwiches, and everything that an authentic ice cream truck may have had. It even played, out of two twelve-inch Pioneer subwoofers, the classic tune that had been luring little children for generations.

"Hey, daddy, can I give you something to lick on?" Promise asked Ox as she leaned over toward him and slowly licked her lips.

"Just give me one of those Oreo cookie sandwiches and unlock the back door," Ox replied.

"That's y'all transport?" Fifteen asked Pain with an astonished look on his face.

"Hell yeah! How many times you ever seen an ice cream truck get pulled over by anybody who didn't want some ice cream?" Pain reopened the trunk of the Acura and transferred the cocaine into the truck.

"Cuzo, with y'all planning, you niggas are gonna be selling my weight soon! I gotta give you credit where credit is due. I ain't expect for y'all to be moving like this." Fifteen gave Pain some dap as he looked over the truck. "Shit, y'all even got ice cream in this bitch!"

"Daddy, I gots to use the bathroom," Promise said to Ox in her innocent little girl voice.

"We ain't got time for that shit right now, girl. You got moves to make. Why didn't you take your ass to the fuckin' bathroom before you got here?" Ox spoke harshly to Promise, loud enough for Fifteen to hear but not enough to make a scene.

"I didn't want to be late. Last time I was late, you got really mad, and I didn't want to get in trouble." Promise rocked back and forth on her feet behind the ice cream truck just like a child in need of a potty.

"Well, you got to hold it or piss on yourself!" Ox was showing no compassion for her need to relieve herself.

"But, daddy, it's gonna be another two hours before I get back out to Mount Dora. I can't wait." Promise damn near broke into tears.

"Cuzo, if you want, little mama can use the bathroom inside the house," Fifteen said to Ox, feeling sorry for the girl. "You damn sure don't want her to stop at no gas station to piss with that shit up in there."

"You right. Appreciate that. Fucking around with her, I might catch a damn charge. Go ahead and use the bathroom, and hurry up. We ain't trying to be out here all goddamn day!" Ox ordered as Promise damn near ran to the house.

Fifteen couldn't help but notice Promise's round ass bounce as she hurried up the driveway to the front door. The way that her ass jiggled with every step, he was more than positive that she didn't have on any underwear. If he looked hard enough, he could probably see through the yellow sundress that she was wearing. Realizing that the front door was still locked, he walked up there to open it before she pissed on herself.

Pain could see Fifteen's eyes follow Promise and knew that his plan was coming together perfectly. He took that moment and had a few words with Real, who gave him a rundown on what he saw earlier. After hearing about Flaco's secret room, Pain quickly decided that it was time to cash in.

"Thank you for letting me use your bathroom. I would never have made it all the way back to Lake County," Promise said to Fifteen as she walked out of the bathroom.

"Ain't nothing, little mama. I just wasn't trying to have you suffer the whole drive back and risk you peeing on yourself." Fifteen was getting a bottle of water out of the refrigerator when she walked into the room. Just as he thought, he could see straight through the yellow sundress as she walked right up to him.

"At least somebody knows how to treat a woman around here. That nigga only care about his money and his cars." Promise touched Fifteen on his chest as she spoke to him.

"Shit, I thought y'all two was tight. You calling him daddy and everything." Fifteen could see her nipples through her dress as her hand slid down to his stomach until it reached the handle of the 9 mm Glock he had concealed in his waist.

"We tight, I guess. He takes care of most of my needs when it comes to money, but sometimes a bitch needs a little bit more." Promise bit softly on her bottom lip as her hand slid down to his dick. "Diamonds aren't the only best friend this girl has."

"Li'l mama, you is trippin'. Your man is outside waiting for you." Fifteen's dick was as hard as Chinese arithmetic as Promise unzipped his pants and pulled his dick out and began stroking it. "We ain't got no time for this right now."

"There's always time for what you want." Promise bent over and circled the head of Fifteen's dick with her tongue before taking it deep in her mouth. She worked her mouth furiously around his dick before she took it out. "Baby, just make sure you don't shoot me with nothing but cum."

Caught up in the moment, Fifteen took his gun and put it on top of the refrigerator while Promise slid out of the sundress and bent her naked body over the kitchen counter. Within moments, Fifteen felt the warm, wet lips of her pussy wrap around his dick as his hands firmly gripped her ass cheeks. After long strokes and watching her ass slam back and forth into his waist, he found himself covered with Promise's juices. She reached around and pulled his dick out before he could get a chance to cum, and she redirected it into her ass. Fifteen was shocked as he watched her lick her own nipple as she took him deep in her sphincter, and with her free hand she took two fingers and rubbed her clitoris. Feeling himself about to cum, Fifteen was on the tips of his toes while he fucked Promise, trying to push his balls inside of her. Being a pro at what she did, Promise knew by the throbbing of the Tampa boy's dick inside of her that he was about to cum, so it was time to put the icing on the cake. She spun around and took his dick deep to the back of her mouth as he shot his thick load down her throat. Just like a pro, the super freak sucked every drop of semen and used the tip of her tongue to lick from the tip of his dick to the scrotum. Fifteen felt shivers up his spine as he found himself in a state of euphoria, oblivious to anything besides the nympho on her knees in front of him.

"Did you like that, daddy?" Promise said, still holding his dick up against the side of her face.

"Damn, girl, you are something serious!" Fifteen said while trying to catch his breath. "I'm daddy already? You better not let buddy hear that."

"Don't worry, homie. She was talking to me. Ain't that right, baby girl?" From behind Fifteen, Ox's voice came as a surprise, causing him to jump.

"Who else I'm gonna call daddy? This fool didn't last five minutes." Promise took Fifteen's now-flaccid dick and tossed it to the side as though it was a cigarette butt. Picking up her dress, she spit the cum that remained in her mouth onto the floor.

"Goddamn, cuzo, she jumped on the dick. I tried to tell her to chill, but she wasn't trying to hear it." Fifteen turned around to see Ox, Pain, and Real standing there. The sound of Ox cocking a pistol-grip shotgun made him instinctively reach for his waist for the gun that was no longer there.

"This ain't about no pussy, Cuzo. It's way bigger than that. First, I want you to walk slowly back over to the bathroom." Ox used the nozzle of the shotgun to direct Fifteen.

Obediently, Fifteen walked into the bathroom with the three men behind him. His own speech about getting priorities in order came back and bit him in the ass. He slipped big time by putting a piece of pussy between himself and a nigga who had just dropped 250 stacks with no problem. With the barrel of the shotgun, Ox pushed Fifteen toward the bathtub and told him to get in and sit down. Silently, he cursed Bezo for not being there today of all days. There would be no way these niggas would have gotten the drop on him if Bezo were there. In his mind, all these niggas did was pull out a shotgun and had his people's champ scared to death. He probably gave up his gun, too.

"Cuzo, this ain't gotta get that serious. We got plenty of money to get together. If I knew she meant that much to you, I swear to God I wouldn't have touched her." Sitting in the tub, Fifteen was trying to resolve the situation that he thought he was in.

"Look here, homebody, I done told your little ass before that this ain't about her! Right now the best thing for you to do is sit back and listen to my partner over here," Ox said through clenched teeth with the barrel of the shotgun trained on Fifteen's face.

"Check this out, son. This shit can be as simple as you make it, or it can get rougher than you can handle. It is your choice. I hope that you use your brain and decide to make it simple." Pain put one leg up on the edge of the bathtub, brandishing in his hand a .45-caliber Glock. "You got something that I need," Pain stated. "All you have to do is give it to me and we'll be going back to our side of town."

"What? You mean this is about money? I thought y'all was about making major paper. There ain't no cash here. Only the money y'all just paid me. Ask your boy over there. If you want it, it's still in the book bag right on the kitchen table." Fifteen began to babble.

"Naw, son, I'm after a much bigger prize. That cash is for you. I want you to give me access to that club you took Real to earlier. I hear that it got more in it than what the fucking *chico* even deserves," Pain said in a calm voice.

"Give you access to Flaco's club? I don't get it. It's just a strip club. It ain't no private country club." Fifteen's dumb response was already anticipated by Pain.

"Real, I want you to tell your boss man exactly what the fuck is going on! In about ten minutes that front door is going to open, and I don't think he's gonna like it." Pain looked at his watch as he spoke to his ex-cellmate.

"He ain't dumb by a long shot. He know we don't want to go to the club for no goddamn music. Just for the fuck of it I'll spell it out. We want the cash!" Real said as he leaned on the doorway.

"You know I ain't got no control over that shit! That's Flaco's shit! How can I get that for you?" Fifteen came to realize that Real was nothing but a spy for the enemy. "Damn, how you gonna do me like this when I was treating you so good? That nigga Bezo was right all this time. I'm willing to bet he's gonna show up and make sure you niggas rise up out of here!"

"How about betting your life on it?" Pain pulled something out of his pocket and dropped it in Fifteen's lap. "I see now that instead of this being simple, we gonna have to make it rougher than you can handle!"

Fifteen picked up the object and instantly knew that the cavalry would not be coming to save the day. In his hand he held the rose gold Cuban link with the 813 diamond pendant that Bezo had custom-made. Either way it went, Fifteen knew that his life was going to come to an end, whether it be at the hand of Pain's crew, or Flaco and his brothers sending his body parts to his mama's house. His thought was interrupted by the voice of the bitch who distracted him long enough for these niggas to get in his house.

"Daddy, the other car is outside. You want me to leave or what?" Promise asked from the doorway of the bathroom.

Before Ox could answer, Fifteen made an attempt to grab the shotgun, only to receive a stiff left hook by Pain. With his hand still holding the barrel of the shotgun, the Tampa boy fell back into the tub, pulling Ox in with him. With Ox off-balance, Fifteen tried to disarm him. Although his jaw felt like he was just hit with a cinderblock, he knew this was a struggle that his life depended on. Suddenly the three-round burst of an MP5 shattered the shower tiles right above Fifteen's head, leaving his face covered with fragments of ceramic. With brute force, Ox drove his fist into Fifteen's nose, causing him to lose his grip on the shotgun. Through teary eyes, Fifteen looked up at his attackers, expecting for his life to be over, only to find out that there were two other men in the room.

"Ah wha gwan in yah so? You mean fi tell mi she all a uno in yah and one man a give you so much trouble, ah must a Hercules this." Reef stood behind Ox, holding the MP5 and laughing as he made his presence known.

"My nigga, I suggest you open your mouth with all the right things I wanna hear or it's gonna be a long night!" Pain said to Fifteen while screwing a silencer on his .45.

"I told you I can't get nothing out of there. If you want it, go get it your fucking self!" Fifteen answered, deciding that if he was to die, it would be as a soldier.

"Mek we talk to da yout fi a likkle while, me sure she him ah go change him mind." Reef leaned forward toward Fifteen, smiling.

"Fuck you and the rest of y'all niggas! You might as well do what you do, pussy motherfuckers. Ain't no bitch-made nigga you fucking with!" Fifteen yelled in Reef's face.

"Well, all right, if you nuh whan chat to mi, I gwan let mi bredren Dummy deal wit' de case." Reef stepped away from the tub just as Dummy shot Fifteen with a Taser gun, causing Fifteen's body to tremor and shake. Pulling out a set of handcuffs, Dummy secured Fifteen to the faucet of the tub by his wrist.

The mute left the bathroom for about two minutes and returned with a deadly surprise for the prisoner. Pain whispered to Reef that he wasn't ready to kill the Tampa boy yet, but he wanted the necessary details of Flaco's club at all costs. Fifteen regained consciousness, and his heart damn near stopped beating when he saw what the sadistic Dummy had planned for him. His loyalty to Flaco and upholding the G-code that he tried to maintain was about to fly out the window.

"All right, now, if any of uno frighten of a little blood, you better left ya so," Reef said to the rest of the crew.

"Shit, I gotta see this shit! Daddy, can I stay and watch?" Promise sat down on the bathroom sink, watching Dummy prepare his torture device.

"You are one sick puppy, baby girl. You'll probably cum on yourself watching this shit. It's up to Reef and Dummy. I'm going in the other room because I know I don't wanna see this." Ox walked out of the bathroom with the shotgun resting on his shoulder.

"All right, lady love, just sit back and enjoy the stage show. Ay bwoy Mr. Dummy ah go show yow a scene from him favorite movie. Mi know sey you done seen *Scarface.*" Reef's words were barely heard by Fifteen because of the roar of the small gas engine that was attached to the buzz saw that Dummy just started up.

CHAPTER SEVENTEEN

"Wha ya sey deh, bwoy? It come in like you no know she ah serious ting we a deal wit'. You no know fi speak English or wha?" Reef mocked Fifteen's cries of agony as Dummy barely pressed the chainsaw to his stomach enough to cut him.

"They must really be important to you or you just plain stupid. You think they would go through this shit for you?" Promise asked as she sat on the sink watching Fifteen squirm on the bottom of the bathtub.

"You know wha, Dummy? Mi think the bwoy feel sey a play we ah play wit' him," Reef said as he pulled out an ice pick from his back pocket. "Turn off dat ting and hold him foot straight."

As his partner suggested, Dummy laid the saw on the ground and grabbed Fifteen's legs and secured them in his tight grip. Promise was amused by the torture tactics of the Jamaicans and how calm they remained as they delivered them. Reef and Dummy didn't flinch or show any remorse for their victim. In fact, they looked like it was all innocent fun to them.

"Now if you kick you foot an' mess up mi friend hand, it ah go be pure worries fi you." Reef took the ice pick and penetrated Fifteen's skin over his shin bone. Moving his hand back and forth, Reef used the tip of the sharp tool to scrape Fifteen's shin bone, causing him agonizing pain. With his legs caught in the vise-grip clutch of Dummy, his only defense was to give in to the demands of his captors. Flaco was on his own to defend his treasure. These niggas were definitely making things harder than he could handle.

"You sure them dudes ain't kill him in there, son? I don't hear no more screaming. They may have cut that nigga to pieces," Ox said to Pain out in the living room.

"Don't worry. One thing about them niggas is they are efficient like a motherfucker. I told them not to kill him, so he should be all right," Pain responded while flicking the ashes off his Black & Mild on the floor, hoping that he was right.

"I'm glad you got them niggas under control, because I only thought white people was into chopping motherfuckers up and shit." Real sat with his gun in his lap, waiting to see what happened next. "At least y'all let the little nigga get some pussy first."

The attention of the three men turned toward the sound of the bathroom door swinging open as Fifteen fell into the room with his hands cuffed behind his back. Pain silently sighed in relief that the Tampa boy was still alive, and the fact that he was in front of him could only mean that he was ready to cooperate. It was beginning to look like he was going to have to settle for the twenty kilos already in the van. Even though that was already a hell of a come-up, Pain wanted the much bigger prize.

"Well, boss man, my bwoy sey him haf sumting fi chat wit' you about." Reef stepped over Fifteen's body and sat on the arm of the couch.

"I'm glad that you had a change of heart. I told you this shit can be simple," Pain said with a smile on his face as he noticed the fresh wound on the captive's stomach and the blood flowing down his leg. "Now let's start with the basics, and please don't leave anything out."

"When I tell you all of this shit, you might as well go ahead and kill me because I'm a dead man anyway," Fifteen said through the pain burning his stomach. His flesh was torn across his abdomen in a gash about nine inches wide and half an inch deep. Every breath he took made it feel as though it were ripping wider open.

"Listen, little man, I'm a fair guy. Tell me the whole scene, and not only will I let you keep that knapsack, but I'll let you keep them twenty bricks that's out in the truck. That's only if I see results, of course!" Pain looked Fifteen square in his watery eyes as he made him the offer that he really had no choice but to accept.

"You gonna let me keep all of this shit? Something don't sound right about this deal. There has to be more to this shit." Fifteen couldn't understand Pain's motive at all.

"It's just my way of showing appreciation for all the hospitality you've showed me and my peoples here," Pain said, patronizing the man on the ground. He already knew that Fifteen's life probably wasn't going to last another twenty-four hours, so why not make a few empty promises to pacify him? "What should matter to you right now is that what I'm giving you will be enough for you to get on track somewhere else, plus you'll be alive."

"Hey, baby girl, go and get a towel from the bathroom so that my man over here don't bleed to death. See if you can find some peroxide or something. You know we got to take care of our host," Pain said to Promise.

"Y'all working a bitch all around the board today! Next thing you'll be asking me to cook dinner, too," Promise said as she rolled her eyes and marched to the bathroom.

"Now that we got that shit out of the way, talk!" Pain leaned forward, giving Fifteen his undivided attention.

For a multimillion-dollar operation, Flaco's setup was just as simple as a local trap house.

Fifteen knew just about everything that Pain wanted to know about the contents in the secret room and the in-house security working for him. As Pain expected, Flaco had paid protection at the club. For twenty grand a week, the two officers who worked the area would make sure that the cars that came from and went to the club would not be hassled or pulled over for probable cause. This way no one would have to worry about catching a trafficking charge if they got some work from Flaco. Little did Flaco expect that his courtesy for his customers was going to help the New York crew get in and out without worrying about getting stopped by the police. The only complicated part was getting into the stash room. The two switches used to open the door were only known by Flaco himself. If the wrong switch was triggered, it would send out a silent alarm to his personal henchmen as well as his police protection. So not only did they have to get one of Flaco's guys to open the door, they also had to make sure that none of the alarms would go off. The plan was now crystal clear: neutralize Flaco's personal security, keep anyone from running out, get Flaco to open the vault, and don't let anyone set off the alarm. Whether they accomplished all of these things or not, two things were guaranteed: danger and destruction.

"That's all there is to it? You wouldn't send me on any kamikaze suicide mission, now would you?" Pain asked Fifteen for the final time.

"Cuzo, this whole thing is a suicide mission. You really think you just gonna walk in there and get that motherfucker to open his stash room for y'all niggas? Them *chicos* is ready for war up in that motherfucker! With all the hired guns he got, you'll be lucky to get away with not leaving a tip for the bartender," Fifteen said as Promise removed the blood-soaked towel from his stomach.

"You dead right, little man, ain't no way he gonna open it just like that for no strangers. That's why you and your people's champ Real are going back to make sure it gets opened." Pain signaled Reef to take the handcuffs off the hostage.

"Hold on, this wasn't a part of the deal! I can't go up in there with y'all. Those *chicos* know where my mama stay at and everything. I'll be a dead man for sure!" Fifteen panicked at the thought of getting deeper into this shit.

"Right now you need to worry about us, not them. Unless you wanna end up like your friend Bezo with your head cut the fuck off, I suggest that you untuck your tail from your fucking ass and get ready, because tonight we are fucking clubbing!" Pain stood over Fifteen, giving his final ultimatum with Ox at his side with his shotgun trained at the Tampa boy's face. "Any more fucking questions?"

With his hands now free, Fifteen sat on the chair with a fresh towel pressed against his stomach. His leg wasn't bleeding as much as when he initially got punctured with the ice pick, but it still hurt like hell. He sat and thought about the situation that he was in, hoping to still get out of it alive. His mind ran across Bezo, and he wondered if he really got his head cut off like Pain said. Across from him sat Dummy, who seemed like a well-trained watchdog, never taking his eyes off of Fifteen just in case he tried to do something foolish. At this point there was no more fight in the Tampa boy. He just sat there listening to Pain orchestrate his plan with the rest of his crew. By the way things were sounding, he just might pull it off.

CHAPTER EIGHTEEN

"All I get is one bullet? What the fuck am I going to do with this?" Fifteen examined the clip that Ox handed to him.

"Nigga, you better use it on the right motherfuckin' one! You think we gonna give your ass enough bullets to turn on us? Pain might be crazy enough to let you carry, but I'm not gonna put too much faith in you!" Ox said as he put his shirt on over his Kevlar vest.

"When shit pops off, the smartest thing you can do is hit the floor. If you want, you can put that bullet in your own fucking head," Real said to Fifteen while securing the extended clip in the MAC-90.

"Y'all niggas ease up off of the little man. He don't want no trouble. We gonna get paid together. Ain't that right, homie?" Pain said as he handed Fifteen his own Glock 17.

"You sure you wanna put that much trust in this nigga?" Ox questioned Pain.

"Dawg, if this nigga decides that he wanna do something stupid and get killed instead of getting paid, that's on him. Besides, we want to make sure our little homie is comfortable." Pain winked as he spoke to Ox. "How's that stomach feeling?"

"Them crazy dreads put a goddamn chainsaw on it! How you think it's feeling?" Fifteen said as he examined the bloody bandage his captors had put on him.

"If it were up to me, I would have cut your whole goddamn leg off, so stop fucking whining." Ox wasn't really feeling Pain's plan on taking this nigga along with them, but he was the only way to get Flaco to open that damn room. As soon as it was over, Ox had plans to personally get rid of the Tampa boy with or without Pain's approval.

"All right, son, let the little nigga breathe for now. We got a long night ahead of us. Real, go and grab this nigga some clean clothes out of the closet or something so it won't look like little homie has been working in a slaughterhouse all day," Pain said as he retrieved his BlackBerry from his pocket to check on Reef and Dummy. To draw less suspicion, he sent the island boys to the club to get a good position on Flaco's goons just in case things got ugly.

"Shout!" Reef answered his phone.

"What's good, son?" Pain could hear the club music coming through the phone.

"Nuff niceness ah gwan in ah de place. Mek haste an pass tru da area." It took a second for Pain to interpret Reef's native tongue, but he knew everything was a green light. Without another word, he hung up the phone and was ready to get on the road to riches.

"What I don't understand is how this *chico* don't have any metal detectors at the door. He must really think that he is untouchable," Ox said to Real as he checked the clip to the Mini-14 in his lap.

"He got some spot checkers, but they really don't even fuck with nobody. His reputation alone keeps anybody from trying to do anything crazy. The last fool who got out of line in there got accidentally shot in the face at the bar by one of the cops on his payroll," Fifteen said, hoping that maybe there would be a spark of fear in the conspirators.

"I wouldn't give a fuck if he had a reputation for shitting cake and pissing champagne. This motherfucker is going to get touched tonight! We going to put the big guns by the service entrance and walk through the front door with the handguns. Reef is already there by the door, so it won't be a problem getting them inside." Pain tucked in his Desert Eagle and put an extra clip in his pocket. "Now, if you ladies are ready, it's time to get paid! Remember, if we get the cocaine, it's all right, but we have to get the money first!" Pain reminded his troops before walking out the door.

"We got you. The money is really the only thing I'm concerned with. It's gonna be hard as hell to haul all that dope out of there anyway. Wait until you see the shit," Real said as he grabbed the duffel bag full of artillery and threw it over his shoulder.

"Shit, with all the work we put in this shit, we might as well get all we can," Ox commented as he made his way to the front door.

"We gonna get all we can, but I don't want us to get greedy and cause complications. We make one trip in and out, and whatever we can't carry we leave. Everybody straight?" Pain said as he blocked the door to make sure everyone knew their position before going any farther.

"I been ready for this shit since I got to Florida, my nigga! Them pussy crackers done sent a nigga up the road for some bullshit. It's time to get my forty acres and a mule." Real patted the Calico that was concealed under his shirt.

"All right. Real, you take this little nigga in the Acura, and me and Ox are gonna follow behind in the Skyline," Pain said. "If you get any ideas of doing something dumb, get it out of your mind, little nigga, because if that car so much as swerves, we're gonna pump so many motherfucking bullets in that shit, by the time the car stops nobody will recognize who the fuck was in it!"

"It's too late for threats. I can't put up no fight now. I'm with y'all niggas. I wish y'all had told me about the two hundred and fifty stacks and the twenty bricks before y'all got all medieval on me with that ice pick," Fifteen said, admitting that he might as well join the stronger team.

"I told y'all this little nigga was gonna come around to his senses. We just gonna chill and ride. Ain't that right, little homie?" Fifteen had no choice but to give an obedient nod and half a grin as Real spoke.

"Y'all slippin' already. You forgetting to bring this for the *chico*. Tighten up!" Pain said as he tossed the book bag full of counterfeit money at Fifteen's feet. "We don't want no unnecessary problems, so make sure you pay him for the twenty bricks first. This way he won't have beef in coming off of the product."

"I told you, this nigga's mind is like that cracker Hannibal on *A-Team*. Always got a master plan," Real joked as they walked to the cars in the drive-way.

Getting in the Acura's passenger seat, Fifteen could feel the tense stare of Ox penetrating his face. Between him and the Jamaicans, he couldn't tell who was more dangerous. All he could hope for was that Pain and Real wouldn't leave him alone with either of them, or else he would be as good as dead. They'd already proved that they were playing for keeps by killing his right-hand man. Now these niggas were minutes away from running up in the club of one of Florida's strongest drug dealers to just take what they wanted. Either they were incredibly brave or just flat-out had a death wish. No matter which one it was, Fifteen was now caught smack in the middle of it. The profit he made, if he survived this, he'd have to use to move away and buy himself a whole new life just because he got caught in a game of high risks.

"Just relax. Everything gonna be straight from here on out." Real's voice broke Fifteen's thoughts.

"Huh? Yeah, cuzo, I'm straight. I was just thinking . . ." Fifteen said softly.

"Naw, bro, don't think. We gonna do all the thinking from now on. It's the safest thing you can do right now—do your part and get paid. Otherwise, shit's gonna really stink," Real said as he pulled out of the driveway, keeping Fifteen in his side view.

"I'm with the program. I'm just hoping for the best. Y'all don't understand what kind of shit we running into. Ain't nobody tried to shortchange Flaco even an ounce, and we about to go and try to take all his shit. At his own stomping ground. That shit ain't gonna be easy as your man back there thinks it is," Fifteen said as he shook his head, looking out the passenger window. He thought maybe he should just put that one bullet in his own head instead of going to a guaranteed bloodbath.

"Listen, nigga, I'm going to tell you something once and once only! That scared shit you talking about is gonna get you in a coffin by your motherfucking self. This *chico* ain't invincible. Even Superman got put in a wheelchair by a fucking horse and now he's dead. This shit is as easy as pie. We go in, lay this shit down, and if a bitch wanna buck, he'll be another fallen hero, bottom line!" Real used a forceful voice to let Fifteen know that it was time to ride or die.

"This is brand new to me. Only thing I know about a jock is trying my best to avoid them. Of all the pistols I had, I ain't never had to bust nobody. That's what I had Bezo for. Not that it matters . . . How did Bezo, you know, how did he die?" Fifteen asked while still staring out the window.

"Truthfully, I wasn't there. I really ain't hear about it until a little while before you found out. I heard about it though, and it was ugly. Put it like this: them dreads must like you, because your head is still attached to your body." Real made a quick glance at Fifteen to make sure he didn't start crying.

"You mean they . . ." Fifteen said as he held his own neck.

"Yup. Straight guillotine action, son. That mute nigga don't fuck around at all. So if you thinking about avenging your homie's death, just look at them little scratches on your stomach and think about what kind of hell they'll put you through," Real said as he saw that Flaco's club was only a few blocks away.

"I'll pass on that. I don't even want to see them niggas again. I just got to make sure his baby mama Angela got what she need for their shortie."

"Yeah, son, you do that." Real didn't bother to tell him that Angela was caught on the chopping block too. "All right, nigga, put your game face on because we almost there. Time to work."

The two men rode down the next two blocks without another word said. Looking over at Real, Fifteen could see that he was calm and cool, while inside, the Tampa boy felt as though his heart might jump out of his chest. It was bad enough that he gave a detailed blueprint of Flaco's operation, but he was being forced to go with the infiltrators. Like he admitted moments ago, he had never shot anyone before because he was protected by his suppliers. Now like an ungrateful dog, he was minutes away from taking a bite out of the hand that had been generously feeding him. Pulling into the club parking lot, he felt as though his legs were made out of spaghetti noodles, and his head started to pound.

"Before we go inside, my man Pain wanted me to give you something to look at," Real said as he pulled out a folded piece of paper and handed it to Fifteen.

Opening the paper up and reading the contents, Fifteen hung his head as though every bit of fight was now completely out of him.

"Come on, cuzo, they ain't got nothing to do with none of this shit," Fifteen said as he held the paper that had the names of his mother and sister with their address.

"Just a little insurance in case you get a sudden change of heart. We hear your old girl is on a dialysis machine. I'm sure you want the best for her." Real had a sly grin on his face.

"Let's get this over with." Fifteen felt the blood flowing through his veins again. If he couldn't get out of doing this, he might as well do it right to make sure these lunatics didn't fuck with his mama. He opened the door of the Acura and stepped out. Out of the corner of his eye, he saw the Skyline pull into the parking lot also.

"That's the attitude you need to have, but before we go inside, smile. We about to enjoy a night at the club," Real cracked as he closed the door of the Acura. He didn't bother to even take the key out of the ignition. He draped a bandana over it to camouflage it. Being an experienced jacker, he knew that when it was time to leave there would be no time to be digging in his pockets to find some keys.

A few yards away, Pain got out of the Skyline and walked to the side entrance and placed the duffel bag with the guns in it behind the trash can. Pain studied the parking lot and could tell that the club had quite a few customers inside. On the way there, they saw Flaco's police patrol sitting a few blocks away with their car idling. As long as this nigga Fifteen didn't nut up under pressure, his crew should be out of there within forty-five minutes. He then saw Real and the Tampa boy enter the club, meaning that in a few minutes they should be in the confines of Flaco's secret room. One thing he did notice was that from the outside of the club he couldn't hear any music because the place was soundproof.

Just then he felt his phone vibrate inside his pocket. He grabbed it and saw that it was Kera. He figured he might as well answer her call now while he still had a chance, or else she'd be blowing him up the rest of the night. With what he was about to do, the last thing he needed was to be worrying about his girl calling back-to-back.

"Hi, babe," Pain answered nonchalantly. "What's up?"

"Hey, nothing much. Just checking in on you," Kera replied. "How was the meeting?"

When Pain was getting ready to leave the house, he had told Kera that he was going to meet with a new potential business partner. The thing was that Pain had been lying to Kera about what he was really up to. Pain would sometimes feel bad about lying to her, but he justified it by convincing himself that he was technically telling the truth. He was just choosing to tell her only the things he wanted her to know.

The thing was, he had promised Kera that he was done working in the streets and he was going to stay on the straight and narrow this time around. Kera had told him that she wouldn't stay with him if he continued to get caught up doing illegal things. She loved him through anything and no matter what, but with them having Junior, she had to think with her head and not her heart. She had to do what was best for her and her son as far as their lives and safety were concerned. She also didn't want Junior to grow up having to see his father in and out of jail all his life. That was not a good example for him.

Pain understood and respected where she was coming from, but what she didn't understand was how hard it was for a man to get back on his feet and get his life together after spending years in prison. It was easy for people to speculate and assume that they would do better if they were in the same position, but things were always easier said than done. When he was locked up, the world kept going without him. But while the world was moving on, Pain felt like he was frozen in a time loop. It was the same shit every day. The only thing that changed was the food in the cafeteria. Other than that, it was like he was living in a bubble. There were not many ways to keep up with what was going on out in the world, so by the time he got released, he was out of touch with the world. While he was stuck on the inside, frozen in time, things changed. Technology was updated, businesses had grown and died or evolved. It was hard out here when he came out.

Now Pain tried in the past to stay good, but he didn't have time to spend years saving his money just to still not be able to afford to pay for things for himself and his family. It just didn't feel right if he was not able to buy gifts for his girl on their anniversaries or her birthday. He also knew he had to make sure she and Junior were always taken care of. It was bad enough that money had started to run out in the last year of his sentence. It killed him that Kera had to start working to keep up with bills. He never wanted his girl to ever have to worry about paying for anything.

Growing up, he and his brother always saw their mom working and stressed out just to keep the lights on and keep a roof over their heads. She somehow always made sure they had decent food to eat in the house, but they did eat a lot of sandwiches and cereal.

"The meeting went well," Pain explained. "He actually wants us to meet up with another potential investor. I'm getting ready to meet with the guys right now, matter of fact," he continued with his lie.

"Oh, wow, that's great news." Kera was truly happy for him. She had been hoping that things would continue to go well for Pain. "Do you think you'll be home in time for dinner, or should Junior and I eat without you?" she asked.

"No, you two go ahead and eat without me." Pain started walking back toward his car. "I'm most likely going to get home late tonight. It seems like these guys might take a little more convincing to win over the contributions." Pain was technically not lying. He was in fact getting ready to head into a meeting where they'd be taking money from the *chico* so they could invest in themselves. He was just cleverly leaving out the part that stated that the money was illegal and it was coming from drug dealers.

"Oh, okay. If that's the case, then I'm not going to bother to cook. I'll just tell Junior to order some Chinese food. I've been craving chicken wings and pork fried rice."

"Okay, beautiful. Order whatever food you like," Pain said as he sat back in the car and took a look around the parking lot. "I'm about to head inside, and I don't think I'll have any reception." He figured if he told her there wasn't reception, she wouldn't be trying to call or text him for a little bit.

"All right. Good luck with the meeting. I'll talk to you later," Kera replied nonchalantly. She had no idea of the major operation her man was about to pull off on the other end.

CHAPTER NINETEEN

Kera hung up the call with Pain. He sounded excited about this meeting, but she couldn't make out if it was good excited or bad excited. For the last few days, something had felt off with him. She didn't want to admit it, but she felt like he wasn't being honest about something. She couldn't pinpoint if he was straight-up lying to her or if it was something else. Call it women's intuition, but she definitely could feel a burning in her stomach that could only be an indication that something was happening.

"Mom, are you okay?" Junior startled her and snapped her thoughts back into reality.

"Yes, I'm okay. I was just thinking about something." She shook her head and smiled up at her handsome son. She couldn't help but notice how much he was looking like his father nowadays. "I just got off the phone with your dad. He's going into a meeting, so he won't be home until later tonight. Do you want to order some Chinese food?"

"Ooh, yes!" Junior was more than happy for them to be ordering Chinese food. It was one of his favorites. "I was coming to ask if you wanted to watch a movie with me tonight. I'm done with my homework, and I feel like I haven't spent too much time with you lately."

Kera was so touched that her son was asking her to do a movie night. She was grateful to see that he was trying to change his attitude with her. Ever since that night that the three of them had their outburst, it seemed like everyone was trying to do their best to keep a good atmosphere in the house.

"That sounds like such a good idea," Kera replied to him. She took his order down and grabbed the phone to call their favorite Chinese spot, Jacky's Kitchen, so they could order for delivery. She didn't feel like driving anywhere tonight. Just as she had the phone in her hand and was about to dial out, her screen lit up. She looked down and noticed it was Mama Phillips calling her.

"Hi, Mama," Kera answered. "*Bendicion,*" she added, which meant, "Blessings." Kera always blessed her elders whenever she saw or spoke with them as part of her Puerto Rican culture.

"Hi, honey. Bless you too. How are you doing?" Mama Phillips asked. Over the years, Mama Phillips had grown used to a lot of Hispanic customs that she had learned with Kera.

"I'm good. I was just getting ready to order some dinner for Junior and me. Your son has been out all day trying to work out some business deals and won't be coming home until late, so Junior and I are doing Chinese food and a movie."

"That sounds wonderful," she responded. "I just woke up from a nap."

"A nap? It's almost nighttime," Kera chuckled.

"Who you telling? I got back from visiting a friend of mine, and I felt tired, so I decided to have a seat on the couch and close my eyes for a few minutes. Next thing I know, two hours have passed and I'm still sitting on the couch with my shoes on and everything. I still have my purse sitting next to me."

"Oh, man, you must've been really tired to have fallen asleep like that," Kera said.

"I was. But guess what I dreamt of during my nap," Mama Phillips said excitedly.

"I haven't the slightest clue," Kera said. "Was it a good or bad dream?"

"Well, that depends on how the person will feel about it." Mama explained, "I dreamt of fishes."

Immediately Kera knew where Mama Phillips was going with this. "Oh, no. You're not bringing that to me. It's not me. Lord knows now is not the time for that," Kera tried explaining herself to Mama Phillips.

Mama Phillips was old-school, and she came from a culture that had what people nowadays called old wives' tales. Supposedly, when an elder dreamt of fishes, it was because someone was pregnant. Mama Phillips dreamt of fishes, so she was hopeful that it meant Kera was pregnant with her second grandchild.

As much as Kera would have loved to have another baby with Pain, now was not the best time. Pain had just gotten out and was trying to build his business from scratch. Junior was still adjusting to his dad being home and also adjusting to this new phase of adolescence he'd stepped into. Kera was focusing on her own things and trying to figure out what direction she wanted her life to go in. Getting pregnant and having a baby would force her to put her life on hold again. She loved being a mom, but it really took a lot of work and sacrifice. When Junior was born, she stopped going to school. She had her associate's and was working on her bachelor's when she found out she was pregnant. Pain stepped up and started working the streets more so they could be ready and have extra savings on the side for when Junior was born.

Pain didn't want Kera to have to work or worry about anything except taking care of herself and his seed. Everything was good for the first few years, but that was when the law started catching up to Pain and he started going back and forth, doing small sentences that lasted a few months here and there. The good thing was that Pain had money set aside for the months he wasn't working, so either way Kera and Junior were always taken care of. Things changed when he got arrested this last time and he ended up having to do a few years. Their savings really dwindled during that time. Kera picked up a full-time job over this last year to keep up with things. Now that Pain was home, she wanted to take some time to focus on herself and decide what it was she wanted to venture into. She also wasn't even sure if she wanted to have another baby after all these years.

"I'm only telling you what I dreamt about. Don't shoot the messenger," Mama Phillips giggled. "Ooh, I'd be so excited to have another little one running around. A little baby girl so we could do her hair and dress her up."

"I bet you'd love that, wouldn't you?" Kera smiled. It made her happy to hear Mama so giddy and excited. She sounded like a little child talking about dressing up and playing with her doll.

"Okay, Kera, well, I won't keep you on the phone so you can go ahead and place your food order. You two go and have a good night. Give Junior a kiss for me." Pain's mom and Kera said their goodbyes.

Kera placed the order, except she decided to pick up the food herself. As much as she didn't feel like driving, she now had a sense of urgency to stop by the Target nearby and pick up a pregnancy test. She really was hoping that she wasn't the fish in Mama Phillips's dream.

CHAPTER TWENTY

"*Que onda vato?* You look like shit, homes," Flaco said to Fifteen as he approached him at the bar.

"A little stressed out, but I'm straight," Fifteen answered, trying to gain his composure. The last thing he wanted was to give himself away by his facial expressions.

"Where's that boy Bezo at? He still missing?" Flaco asked as he waved one of his bartenders over to him.

"Naw, he's at the crib with Angela. The baby is sick, so he's doing the daddy thing right now." Fifteen surprised himself with the quick lie.

"So what's the problem? That ain't no reason to look like you're at a funeral." Flaco looked Fifteen in his eyes to see if he could pick up anything. They say the eyes are the window to the soul.

"It ain't nothing like that," Fifteen said. "One of my bitches just told me that she pregnant from me. I believe the bitch is lying." Once again Fifteen generated a quick lie to get him out of the line of questions.

"Ha, that's all?" Flaco chuckled. "You *morenos* stick your dicks in these skeezers and expect them not to try to get something out of it. These women are gonna say whatever they need to say to get you for your money. You know they gonna make you pay for that pussy one way or another. I promise you she's lying, homes. Pay for her imaginary abortion and give her some shopping money, and then leave her ass alone. Have a drink on me and put that shit out of your mind." Flaco slapped Fifteen on the back, finding his so-called problem amusing.

Fifteen felt the hit on his back and tried not to wince. He was still in pain from the torture and beating he'd gotten earlier.

Flaco poured out three shots from the bottle of Patrón that the bartender brought over, and he set them in front of Fifteen and Real. Turning the glass up to his mouth quickly, Fifteen felt the mellow burn of the liquor going down his throat. Right now he wanted to down the whole bottle to numb his nerves and take away the pain he was feeling. At the same time, though, he knew he couldn't overdo it because he needed to still be alert for what was about to transpire.

By the far corner of the club, he spotted one of the dancers performing for one of the customers. As the girl dropped down low, he saw the face of one of the men who had him at the wrong end of a chainsaw earlier that day, Dummy. Sitting next to him was Reef smoking a cigar with a handful of money. The duo just sat there looking like two guys enjoying a night at the strip club. On the floor between them was the duffel bag of artillery covered up by Dummy's jacket. They were ready for war.

"She's something else, ain't she?" Flaco asked Fifteen, assuming his eyes were locked on the dancer.

"Huh?" Fifteen snapped back to paying attention to the Mexican sitting next to him.

"Her name is Champagne. I gave her the name myself. Pussy so tight it can pop the cork off a bottle of Dom Pérignon," Flaco said as he poured another shot for the trio.

"Yeah, little mama's got one hell of a body on her. I wouldn't mind taking a sip of Champagne later on." Real wanted to take some of the pressure off Fifteen by saying something.

"Let me not make you wait. I'ma let you have a little sippy sip right now." Flaco spun around, raised his right arm, and snapped his fingers as he looked toward where the stripper Champagne was dancing for the Jamaicans. Immediately two other girls walked over toward Dummy and Reef and started giving each of them lap dances. Champagne made her way over toward Flaco and Real.

"Hey, ma. Give my guy here the Champagne Special," Flaco instructed her.

"Nah, man. Let's take care of business first." Fifteen tried to get Flaco to focus. He wanted to get things done and over with.

"Yeah, that's a good idea," Real agreed with Fifteen. "Let's do what we have to do. Work comes before play."

"You guys ain't playing around," Flaco said as he shook his head. "I like the commitment. Go dance in VIP for now." He motioned toward Champagne and waved her off.

Through the entrance of the club, two men walked in and grabbed a seat at one of the tables toward the back near the dancers' dressing room. It wasn't odd for the customers to want to sit back there because of the traffic of girls going in and out of the dressing room. These two had a different agenda though. Pain and Ox were there for the big payoff. Being approached by one of the waitresses, they remained inconspicuous by ordering a bottle of Rémy Martin and 200 singles.

"So, my friend, you going camping or something? What's up with the book bag?" Flaco asked Fifteen just before taking another shot of Patrón.

"This is for you. That deal went through earlier. I came to drop this off, and I need another five of those things," Fifteen answered while shifting his empty glass back and forth.

"You've been real busy, homes, like a little beaver. You working nonstop. I like that you work harder than most *chicanos,*" Flaco said with a laugh as he stood up from the bar. "Let's go to the back to get everything situated."

"You know how I do it! I'm still trying to make up for the lost time I spent in the bin," Fifteen said as he poured himself a third shot and downed it before following Flaco with Real close behind him.

As the three men made their way to the dressing room, Fifteen spotted Pain and Ox sitting at a table being entertained by two dancers. In the back of his mind, he gave them their props for blending into the atmosphere. If he didn't already know, he would never suspect them to be after anything but a good time with the girls. Flaco's goons were relaxed and weren't even picking up on the bad energy among them. They were posted up at the exact spots that Fifteen explained to his captors. With three of them working in the club, the odds were in Pain's crew's favor, and they were prepared to take full advantage of the situation.

"Will you look at this shit! Every time I turn around you two are going at it. You better put that act on the stage and pay your house fees," Flaco said as he entered the dressing room to find Kitten lying on her back with Candy's face buried in her pussy. Even after Flaco slapped Candy firmly on her naked ass, she continued to greedily suck on Kitten's spur tongue, causing her to moan as her back arched off the floor.

"You see what I got to go through around here? I don't know who's hornier—the jokers who throw their rent and car payments on the stage or the freaks who actually work here." Flaco walked over to the fuse box and flipped two switches.

"Yeah, poor you. If you want a vacation, I'll fill in for you for a couple of days," Fifteen said as his eyes were locked on Kitten's legs trembling as she moaned and climaxed in Candy's mouth.

"I bet you would, but it's a burden that I'll have to take all by myself." Flaco winked at the Tampa boy as he spoke.

Fifteen's heart began to pound as he watched the wall mirror slide open. The sudden urge to take a piss was a sure sign that his nerves were shot. As Flaco pulled the light's chain, he wanted to turn around and run, but he knew that he had no place to go. Pain's team was right outside the door with enough artillery to take on a small army. He was stuck. He handed Flaco the knapsack and silently prayed that these niggas he was with were ready for the war they were about to start. On the side of him, Real was as calm as possible waiting for the moment to make the drop on the Mexican.

"*Carajoo!* All of these small bills are gonna be hell sorting out. Next time these *vatos* buy, tell them only big bills. This ain't no goddamn piggy bank!" Flaco said as he emptied the knapsack out on one of the tables in the corner. Before he could turn around, he heard the shrill screams of Candy and Kitten as they got up and ran for the dressing room door.

"What the fuck is wrong with . . ." Flaco swallowed the rest of his question as he turned around to see Real standing a few feet in front of him with the Calico pointed at his head.

"All right, *chico,* I know you're a smart man, so let's both play our parts. Give us what we need, and don't give us any hassle!" Real said as he had a steady grip of the deadly machine with his finger on the trigger.

"You think that toy gonna get you out of here alive, *puto?* Put that thing away, and I'll make sure that my boys don't feed you to the gators." Flaco stared Real down, knowing that once the girls made it to the dance floor, his goons would be rushing in. "And you. You dare disrespect me in my own house? I made you, and now you slap me in the face?" he barked at Fifteen.

Outside the dressing room door, Pain saw the two girls run out buck naked straight to Angelo at the DJ booth. Pain immediately realized it was time to spring into action and pulled his gun out and slipped into the dressing room door. Ox got up to stand by the bar where one of Flaco's goons was posted up talking to one of the dancers working the floor. His hand was resting on the grip of the Colt .44 that was tucked under his shirt. The moment that the short, stocky Mexican made a move toward the back, he planned on putting a slug in the back of his head.

Hearing the frantic explanation of Kitten and Candy, Angelo reached under the DJ console and came up with a pistol-grip pump shotgun and rushed to the back. As he ran toward the dressing room with the shotgun at his side, another dancer was pushed directly into him. Before he could maintain his balance, the report of a MAC-90 echoed through the club, tearing through the dancer and hitting him multiple times in the chest. The last thing he saw was Reef standing over him, pressing the hot nozzle to his face before splattering his skull on the dance floor. With one swift motion, Reef turned the gun on Champagne, who lay on the floor coughing up blood, and delivered two more shots in her chest to put her out of her misery.

Unaware of what was going on in the dressing room, Flaco's goon Antonio reached for the TEC-9 in his waist at the sight of Angelo being gunned down. Before he could take two steps farther, a .44-caliber bullet entered the back of his head and exited through his right eye socket, killing him instantly. Ox quickly scanned the club of screaming dancers and customers for the third hired gun but couldn't spot him until he felt the impact of a sawed-off shotgun slug hit him in the back. The force of the shot threw him off his feet. If it hadn't been for the Kevlar vest that Promise insisted he wear, he would have been one of the casualties of the club. The gunman rushed over to Ox to put a slug in his head only to have his body riddled with bullets by Dummy, who was standing on the stage with flames shooting out of the Mini-14. Within moments, all three of Flaco's henchmen lay in a sticky pool of their own blood, dead.

"Everybody get down pon di blood clot ground!" Reef ordered the whole club, sweeping the area with the MAC-90.

"Make sure that front door is locked so nobody gets up in here!" Ox hollered as he staggered toward the dressing room to check on the rest of the crew. Even though the vest stopped the shotgun slug from tearing a hole through his body, the force of the impact felt like he just took a fierce body shot from George Foreman.

"No bother worry 'bout nuttin' rude body. Any pussy cross dat borderline oh go dead before dem see it!" Reef said as he secured the front door while keeping an eye on everybody lying on their stomachs in the middle of the dance floor.

The sound of a cell phone broke the silence of the club. Looking around, Reef determined that it was coming from the phone hooked on Antonio's waist. With a grin on his face, he turned the MAC-90 toward Flaco's fallen soldier and made his body jump with five rounds.

"Can you hear me now?" Reef playfully said as he continued to perforate Antonio's body. Although he was having fun, he knew the real fun was going down in the dressing room.

CHAPTER TWENTY-ONE

"Where do you think you'll be able to hide once you get out of here, my friend?" Flaco said to his unwelcome guest while lying on his stomach with his hands duct-taped behind his back.

"Check this motherfucker out. He still trying to scare a nigga even after we just manhandled his whole operation in less than ten minutes," Real boasted as he continued to stuff money into the garbage bags.

"I don't know about you, Fifteen, but I can't be looking over my shoulder all my life for no pissed-off *chico* to get his revenge," Pain said as he put his hand on Fifteen's shoulder.

"What . . . what you mean? Y'all ain't gonna let this cat live, are you?" Fifteen asked with a worried expression printed on his face.

"Well, homie, it's like this. Right now each one of us is as dirty as the next in this situation. It's time you earned your merit badge," Pain said as he pointed to the Glock 17 that the Tampa boy had in his waist.

"I . . . I can't kill nobody, man. It's just not me." Fifteen shook his head as he looked down at Flaco.

"Listen, little nigga, who you think this *chico* gonna come looking for first? We ain't the only ones who can find your mama's house," Pain continued to provoke Fifteen.

"You better kill me, *pendejo,* because I swear on your life that when I catch you, I gonna cut off your *pinga* and shove it in your mother's—"

Before Flaco could finish his sentence, a nervous Fifteen drew his gun, cocked the slide back, and put the single shot in the top of Flaco's skull. After the blast, the Tampa boy stood there with his finger still squeezing the trigger as tears began to form in his eyes. Murder was the last thing he thought he was capable of, but he couldn't let Flaco live another day to bring harm to his family.

"Talk that shit now, motherfucker! My boy don't see you homeboy, ha-ha!" Real said as he tied the fourth garbage bag full of cash.

"Don't you feel better now? You ain't got to worry about this fool fucking with you and your people," Pain whispered in Fifteen's ear as he put his arm around his shoulder.

"If y'all niggas are done fucking around, we need to hurry up and get the fuck up out of here," Ox said as he loaded cocaine into the garbage bags.

"Ay, yo, Pain, what the hell them dreads doing out there? I still hear shooting, and all of the *chicos* are down already," Real said, clutching the Calico and rushing to the door.

"Wrap this shit up now. It's time to get the fuck out of here!" Pain said as he grabbed one of the garbage bags while clutching his Desert Eagle with his right hand.

By the time the four men left the dressing room to enter the dance floor, the gunshots had already stopped. Carefully swinging the door open, not knowing what to expect, Pain looked around the club only to see Reef and Dummy sitting on top of the bar, both holding separate bottles of Hennessy. The floor was covered with the bloody bodies of dancers, customers, and employees. Nobody was spared the massacre.

"Whappen, boss? Everything good to go?" Reef asked Pain after taking another swallow of the brown liquor.

"What the hell is this shit?" Pain said as he stepped over body after body.

"You nuh really expect all ah dem people fi keep quiet when de Babylon bwoy dem ask ah who done off Mr. Man and him bredren dem. Plus dem never did wan listen when Dummy tell dem fi stop di noise," Reef joked as he jumped off the bar.

Fifteen felt his stomach doing flips as he looked at the carnage caused by the two Jamaicans. This was all a bad dream that he'd never wake up from. First he lost his partner Bezo, and then he was damn near chopped in half in his own bathtub, and now he was a part of a mass murder. Over his shoulder was the knapsack with the $250,000 worth of counterfeit money while he dragged a bag with another twenty bricks of cocaine. It is said that every man has his price, and Fifteen was paid in full, but he knew that his payment would not prevent the many sleepless nights ahead of him.

"All right, my niggas, let's rise up out of here. Y'all know what to do," Pain said to his crew, grabbing a bag and moving toward the side entrance.

"Shit, the way y'all chilling out here we might as well all get comfortable for a little bit. I think we have a little time to sit around and have some drinks," Ox exclaimed. "Yo, Fifteen, what you want to drink?"

"I'm good," Fifteen replied. He was not in the mood to drink with all these bodies lying around. All he wanted to do was get the fuck up outta dodge.

"Oh, come on. We need to toast. None of this would have been possible without your help and cooperation," Ox said as he grabbed some shot glasses and poured some Hennessy into them. "A toast to my man Fifteen over here. For all his hard work and sacrifice. We thank you for your cooperation." Ox's sarcastic remark was the last thing Fifteen heard before Dummy cut through his face with six shots out of the Mini-14.

"Damn, I was starting to like the little nigga. Oh, well. Two tears in a bucket, fuck it." Real looked down at Fifteen's lifeless body and grabbed the bag that had the cocaine and dragged it to the side entrance.

Within a few moments, Reef and Dummy took the guns and placed them in the hands of the dead club attendees. Arranging their bodies around the club, they made it appear as though the shoot-out had been between the *chicos* and a few patrons. Pain took Fifteen's lifeless body back to where Flaco lay in the secret room and positioned him with the Glock 17 in his hand. Angelo's body stayed where it was, with the Mini-14 replacing the shotgun he once had. After all the bodies were in position, the five men calmly walked into the parking lot with a little more than $6 million in cash and seventy-five bricks of cocaine. The rest of the cocaine was left in Flaco's secret room in order to give the police a sufficient motive for the mass murder. The three cars loaded up and left the scene at a moderate speed. As they drove down the strip, they passed the same patrol car with the two uniformed officers, who appeared to be asleep. For the New York crew, today was turning out to be a very good day.

The next morning, Pain sat at his kitchen table in his Remington-style home, watching the news with his family. The news anchor announced a drug-related club shooting where ninety kilos of cocaine was recovered by investigators. Apparently it was a retaliation led by a Tyrone Hudson, aka Tampa Fifteen, for a gruesome murder and decapitation of his local drug partner Brian Tillman, aka Bezo, and girlfriend Angela Foreman. There were no survivors of the club killing, so no further investigations would follow.

With a smile on his face, Pain reached for his ringing BlackBerry. "What up, son?" Pain answered, seeing Real's number.

"Chillin', homie. You seen the news?" Real said while smoking a blunt.

"Yeah, I seen it. Tragic, ain't it? It's a rough world out there," Pain said, getting up from the table.

"It is what it is. I'm about to take a trip up top for about a week. Let me know what's good when I get back." Real wanted to let Pain know that he was going to vanish for a couple of days.

"I tell you what. In about two days, me and the family are going to Brooklyn to see Mom Dukes. I'm thinking about hitting the ATL scene and trying to get a club scene of my own going on, and I could use some investors. What up, you down?" Pain asked his new partner.

"Well, I think I could scrape up a few dollars to get up with you. Holla at me when you reach up top and we'll hook up. One love, homie." Real hung up the phone and looked over at his share of the heist sitting on the floor next to his bed. $1,200,000 wasn't bad at all for a night's work. The twenty bricks he had would go for the low when he was ready to move it. All in all, he finally got his forty acres and a mule just by playing his part in a game of high risks.

CHAPTER TWENTY-TWO

Pain awoke with a heavy feeling in his chest. He put a hand over his heart, took in a deep breath, and exhaled. Getting out of bed proved to be an extra hard task this morning. Although he had a full night of sleep, his body felt exhausted. For months, Pain had been tossing and turning almost every night having the same dream. It was one of those dreams he remembered intensely and was very vivid. What made things stranger was that up until he'd started having that dream, he never could remember anything he dreamt about. This dream, however, was etched in his memory. He could remember every detail, and everything felt so real.

He swung his legs over the bed, and his feet instinctively fell into his slippers to spare him the shock of the cold floor. Rubbing his eyes, he dragged across the floor with barely enough energy to bend his knees. A little cold water splashed on his face assisted in guiding him back into the reality of the day ahead of him. Looking in the mirror, Pain tried to think past the vivid images that invaded his mind all night that caused him to wake up and second-guess his sanity. No matter how many times he woke up throughout the night though, he'd always go back to the same dream, and it would pick up right where he left off. The shit was just too fucking real.

He could still hear the bloodcurdling screams of the dancer being shot up in the club and could see the looks of terror carved into the faces of those who fell victim to the carnage that had transpired due to his thirst of achieving his goal of claiming what he selfishly considered to be rightfully his. Shaking it off, Pain got a partial grip of his thoughts as he brushed his teeth with what was the last squeeze of toothpaste.

"Today is the day," he whispered to himself. "Sink or swim. I got a lot of catching up to do. It's time to meet the people." Without so much as a knock, the door to his room swung open with his daily "get your ass out of bed" call.

"You eating breakfast this morning, or is your ass in some sort of rush?" The voice coming from the door carried a strong hint of sarcasm, believing that they already knew what answer to anticipate to the unnecessary question.

"I'm gonna eat a little something before I head out of here. I do got a helluva trip ahead of me." Pain's reply came as a shock to the inquisitor at the door of his crowded room.

It took moments for Pain to get ready for breakfast after his daily morning procedures of making sure that he was up and well accounted for, which was so simple it could often become difficult, but no matter what obstacle came his way, big or small, nothing could change the fact that today was the day he took a big step out and into a new place in life. A place that he had been counting down the days to. He had been waiting for so long to finally get to this day.

Pain grabbed his food and found a spot to sit down. He started eating what had become his favorite breakfast of oatmeal and two coffee cakes. Pain could not help but to reminisce about the events of his most recent dream. This was a recurring event that he could never fully get used to. While others saw him as an individual with the precise strategic moves of a great chess player, not too deep within him was a man who was an ant's step away from a full-scale anxiety attack. Keeping his composure was Pain's reputation ever since he adopted the streets into his life, and now was definitely the time to live up to his reputation. After all, according to the interpretation of the books Real had spoken of, reputation was everything, and he needed to guard it with his life, because indeed his life would depend on it no matter what he did.

Finishing up his food as fast as he had grown used to, Pain got up from his breakfast table and proceeded back to his room to gather the belongings he required for his departure.

Never being one to play around in front of the mirror or overpack, Pain was dressed and ready for his trip quickly. The only thing left was for him to get out the front door. No key was necessary, nor was there any reason to check to make sure the stove was turned off. A forwarding address was not needed to be left for the postman because he would never look back to this part of his life again unless it was to be used as a learning reference. It took hard work of being humble and accepting the bullshit of others to reach the position he was in now, and he was ready to grasp life by the fucking neck and live it as he felt fit.

Dressed, with all his belongings, Pain walked to the front office to sign what was similar to a housing lease. He did not expect the return of any security deposit. He just wanted to break all ties with this chapter of his life and start an entirely different book, but always and forever would this experience stay in his head.

He arrived in time to join a line of other residents who were departing to also follow whatever plans they may have made during their stay at the exclusive resort. By the looks and natural body language of the others waiting in the line that seemed to be taking an eternity to move, Pain could pretty much tell who would return to the secluded getaway and who would decide that their time spent there was enough to satisfy any yearning of a return trip.

"Adams! Come forward!" sounded the not-so-pleasant female clerk behind the desk while gathering what appeared to be a file folder containing some papers.

"Ma'am!" responded the anxious tenant as he hurried to the desk as though in a moment she may change her mind and deny him termination of his lease. He went over a few formalities with the clerk that involved applying his signature to a few forms and answering a few questions that confirmed his actual identity.

"Baxton! Come forward!" the clerk hollered as Adams confidently strutted away from her desk with a smile on his face so big that you could see the food caught in his wisdom teeth. The clerk went through the same formalities as she did with Mr. Adams while Mr. Baxton stood there with full cooperation, rocking back and forth in the same manner as a child when they are in desperate need to use the bathroom. His anticipation of departure was evidently very hard for him to contain as he continued to jitter around in what appeared to be a mild seizure caused by excitement.

As Pain watched the others go before him, he contemplated the first steps that he and his bag of luggage were going to make upon his departure when, once again, his mind was invaded by the images of last night's dreams. "Them Jamaicans are crazy as hell," he caught himself murmuring aloud.

"Phillips! Phillips! I ain't gonna sit here calling your fucking name over and over again. Do I have to come around this counter and bitch slap you back to a little place we like to call earth?" The clerk was now standing up and yelling with her chest heaving up and down, causing the metal badge pinned on her chest to appear to come to life with a pulse of its own.

"Feisty as hell today, ain't she?" Pain commented to himself as he took his rightful place.

After approximately one hour, everyone was ready to say their final farewells with sincere hopes of never having the pleasure of seeing one another again. With many alternative ways of leaving, Pain already had a premeditated plan of departure, but just like any other situation in life, anything was bound to happen, so he kept an open mind.

Walking out into the open parking lot, Pain looked around and noticed his partner Real, who shared the same goal of building an empire together, as he entered the passenger side of a 2006 Nissan Altima with who Pain assumed was the woman in his life. Watching him drive off, Pain patted his pocket that held a contact number for

Real, thinking that if he ever had some serious business to handle, he would definitely have to holla at Real. After further investigation of the parking lot, Pain came to the realization that his original plans for departure were in fact the route he was going to take. There was no surprise carriage ride from any unannounced chauffeurs. As he made his way to the Greyhound bus, he could only once again think back to the vivid dream of the preceding night and couldn't help but laugh as he presented his ticket to the bus driver.

Spotting a vacant seat in the rear of the bus, Pain shuffled down the aisle and situated himself next to a gentleman who didn't appear too happy about sharing the confined space of the seats. But by analyzing Pain's body size and natural manner, he found it better to deal with the minor inconvenience than to cause a confrontation that would only lead to his feeble frame being bounced around the bus.

Looking out the window of the bus as the scenery rolled by, Pain focused back on reality and revised some mental notes he had for his arrival to his destination. As a true hustler, Pain already had a connect for when he got there who promised to pay off in what he loved the most: cash! All he had to do was make a phone call and show up to the designated place and the money was a guarantee, which brought him comfort. Anytime the words "money" and "guarantee" were joined in the same sentence, he had no choice but to feel comfortable. Comfortable was a feeling that Pain wasn't sure he'd recognize if he ever felt it.

Because of his environment and having to deal with feelings while standing in crowded rooms, Pain coped by building different realms in his mind. He couldn't allow himself to really let himself feel his emotions or let his thoughts linger too long in the realities of things. In prison, he couldn't be walking around showing emotions. So instead Pain created different scenarios and lifestyles that triggered enjoyment instead of the harsh reality that he really was living in.

Once again, he shook his head as he thought back to the dream that was now the master of ceremonies to the events of his thoughts, and a smile of guilty innocence crept across his face as he thought that no one would believe the shit that transpired in his head. Stephen King would probably pay top dollar for marketing rights to the thoughts that ran through Pain's mind. "Ice cream truck, huh," Pain said to himself loudly enough to make the gentleman on the seat next to him wonder if Pain was indeed talking to himself. Entertaining his thoughts, he sat back and enjoyed the two-and-a-half-hour ride to Orlando.

***

After settling in and taking a shower that seemed overdue by an eternity, Pain gathered up his thoughts while getting dressed for his first stop that just couldn't wait. It was time to get that cash! It all depended on one phone call to a guaranteed connect from a reliable source: his mom. If there was anybody he could always depend on, it was Ma Dukes, so he knew that this would definitely pay off. In return, the least he could do was to treat it as a top priority. This and his natural thirst for money motivated him toward the telephone.

"Hello. Yeah, I would like to speak to a Howard Andrews please," Pain said in his most professional voice to indicate that he was calling to speak about a business matter. "Yes, this is Javon Phillips. My mom, Mrs. Gloria Phillips, told me that you would be expecting my call."

Mr. Andrews was awaiting the call from Pain but didn't know exactly when it would be. He had been a longtime friend of his mom's. They knew each other from a local organization they had both been a part of since Pain and his departed brother were just kids. After speaking for a few minutes, Mr. Andrews and Pain came to an agreement. Their first scheduled meeting was to be the next morning at seven thirty, and if all went well, they'd be continuing to do business with each other for a long time.

Feeling accomplished, Pain concluded his call with the man who now insisted that he call him Howie, and he cradled the bulky phone receiver, thinking that things could only get better from now on. For the first time in a long time, Pain was completely alone, and a strange feeling came over him—a feeling that he had been trying to avoid for about thirty-six months now. The fact was he was finally alone and on his own.

There was no homecoming party, no big, well-furnished home with a loving family waiting for him to get out. No woman waiting to be cuddled up next to him at night and no secret stash of money. The only thing waiting for him and everyone else who walked through the exit doors of any prison was reality, and sometimes that could make the strongest of them all break down. In Pain's case, reality had been something he had been dodging for far too long.

The truth was that after about a year into his prison sentence, Kera decided that him being locked up for so long was too much for her to continue to take on. As much as she tried to go and visit him, she had to work two jobs to keep herself afloat, and between getting time off and being able to pay the travel expenses to get to the prison he was at, it was all too overwhelming. They tried to keep writing to each other and call each other when they could, but they just weren't on the same page anymore.

Then one night, Kera admitted to him that she was falling for someone she had met at one of her jobs. She cried and told him she never meant for it to happen. They had started out as friends. Kera would cry to him about how much she missed Pain, but eventually with them spending so much time together, they started catching feelings. Hearing that broke Pain's heart. He was hurt and angry all at the same time. He felt like Kera had committed the ultimate betrayal. After giving himself a few days though, he realized he couldn't really fault her for finding somebody else. She was young and beautiful. He was the one who had fucked up and ended up in the hellhole. It wasn't fair of him to expect her to put her life on pause for him.

They talked again and he said his piece. After that, they still wrote to each other, but eventually they pretty much fell off. He heard through the grapevine that she had gotten married to the guy and moved to another state. He'd also heard they'd had a beautiful little girl they named Spirit.

Pain thought about the dream he was always having. Man, how nice it would be if he and Kera really had had a baby boy. Pain often thought back to how Kera had an abortion when they were younger. He wondered if maybe the boy Junior from his dream had been the baby they aborted all those years ago. Maybe his dream was like a glimpse of a life he might have had if he had made different choices in his past. Pain was fully aware to not get too stuck on wondering and piecing together events or mistakes from his past. He knew there was no point in staying stuck rethinking how things could have been different. At the same time though, sometimes it was good to look at the past so he could learn from it, make peace with it, and move on.

Pain took a look around the room and took it all in. Lying out on his full-size mattress, he looked up at his ceiling and took a deep breath. He thought about his past life. It was a life that seemed so far away and such a long time ago. It was almost as if it hadn't ever existed if it weren't for the memories he was still holding on to. All he had left were images of a life that was taken from him by the judge and jury, another consequence of his checkered past. He thought again about Kera. For him, she would always be the one who got away. He held no grudge or ill will toward her, and he silently wished her all the best. Man, how nice it would have been if the two of them had really had a little baby boy together.

It was all a dream that came to an end. There was no robbery, no classic cars, no dope, and damn sure there was no money! No submissive women to jump at his command, no up-to-date clothing, and again no fucking money! Pain's mind wandered on many occasions, but this was the most repetitive dream that carried him through his time. Everybody has their share of dreams and this was his. Since the final blow of losing his brother, this was how he did his time. By creating fantasies to detail in his mind. He could still see the image of Fifteen's face exploding, except there was no Fifteen in the first place. Maybe that was for the best, because one thing that was definitely guaranteed was that if he ever went back to doing anything illegal in the streets, the prison system always had a spot for him.

The rest of the night was basically quiet for Pain, which was something that he was definitely going to have to get used to. Falling asleep was harder for him to do in silence than it was with the annoyance of the late-night habits of others. He was also used to hearing keys hit against each other throughout the night as the guards did their rounds and walked around the compound.

The next morning, while still getting accustomed to his new life and surroundings, he laughed as he found himself walking into the shower while still wearing his house slippers. Sometimes routine could force itself on you. The dreams of last night were quite different in comparison to what he had been used to, though. There were no gunshots, whores, or pursuit of fast money. It was all about self-improvement and overcoming the feeling of being alone in a crowd. Most importantly, it was about meeting with his connects and the cash flow that was in store for him.

Before he went to prison, punctuality played a big part in his street hustle. "A nigga who can't be there on time really don't need no money," was his motto then, and he planned to live up to it. So instead of seven thirty, Pain was at the spot at seven fifteen as clean as his wardrobe would allow. Impressed with the humble surroundings of the office, he approached the desk that was positioned within feet of the front door.

"Good morning and welcome to F.D.C. Moving and Storage. May I help you?" The pleasant voice from behind the desk was as sweet as the aroma of the perfume that was worn by the welcoming receptionist.

"Yes, ma'am. I am here to see Mr. Andrews. My name is Javon Phillips," Pain said in a tone to match the sincere voice of the clerk. He was impressed at the professional atmosphere of the spot. This dude Howie was definitely doing his thing! With this kind of setup, Pain knew that getting cash with this dude was going to be a smooth ride as long as he lived up to his end of the bargain, and he had no problem doing that.

In response to a press of a button on the interoffice intercom, a tall dark-skinned gentleman wearing a casual outfit of work boots, jeans, and a button-up shirt emerged from behind a door leading to an adjacent room.

"You must be Javon. Come on in, son, and let me show you around while I tell you the ins and outs of this place," Howie said while greeting Pain with a firm handshake. "I'm sure that it won't be long until you find that, here at F.D.C., we treat our employees just like family. After all, your mom and I had been going to the same church for years until I moved down to Florida. I consider her a church mother to me, so you are like family."

The greeting seemed sincere enough to make Pain feel comfortable in this new environment. The meeting went well, and Pain felt like he was embarking on something that would help him achieve his goals. He wasn't getting himself into a get-rich-quick scheme, and he knew that it was going to take time and serious work to build his status and money, but he had nothing but time in the world. This stint had taken everything and everyone away from him, so he had only himself to work on. It was hard to believe he was completely alone out here, but he was looking forward to reinventing himself and starting fresh.

When the meeting was over, he made his way to visit someone he wasn't ready to see but had to face.

An hour later, he stepped off the bus and started walking a few blocks over to the address he'd been given. He walked around reading the signs until he found what he was looking for.

"Here you are, bruh." Pain looked down and spoke over his brother's tombstone. It felt surreal to be standing over his twin brother's grave. He felt so guilty for not being able to even show up for his burial.

"I can't believe you're gone," Pain said as he felt a pain in his chest. "All my life I had you standing by my side. It's always been you and me through everything. Now I'm back out here, and it just doesn't feel the same that you're not here with me."

Pain looked up into the sky because he felt like his heart was racing. He had told himself that he was ready to come and visit his brother's grave. He hadn't thought about how hard it would be to stand on top of it and finally see it for himself.

"You're going to be proud of me. I'm staying on the straight and narrow side this time. I'm done trying to do my shit in the streets. I'm gonna make you and Mama proud and build my own legal business. I'm even thinking about writing my own book. Shit. With everything I been through I think it would be a bestseller," Pain went on.

"I hate to break it to you, but me and Kera ain't together no more," Pain admitted. It was weird because he hadn't said those words out loud yet. They had broken up while he was incarcerated, but he hadn't really said it to anyone. Up until this moment, the breakup had happened through letters and them not calling each other anymore.

There was never really a moment where they spoke over the phone and made it official.

Pain knew how much his brother cared about Kera. From the first day he introduced them, they had gotten along. He was sure Kera had heard about his passing. He wouldn't be surprised if she had gone to his wake and burial. Kera had always been a good girl like that. She was dependable and caring.

"Man, I really lost a good woman," Pain admitted. "What's sad is everything I was doing was so she and I could have a good life. She kept telling me a good life was one with me and her in it through good times and bad as long as I wasn't caught up in the system. Every time I came home with jewelry or wanted to upgrade her car, she would tell me she didn't care about that stuff and that all she wanted was for me to be safe." Pain paused. "I should have listened to her. She's married to some guy who's got her living out in the suburbs. They have a little girl." Pain felt like he was doing confessions right now, just pouring everything out.

"I ain't mad about it. She deserves nothing but the best. I just wish I had been the man to give it to her," Pain admitted. "It's all good though. I realize now you really do reap what you sow. I just hope somewhere out there I can eventually find my queen and start a family. I promise I'm gonna make you proud, bruh. I'm sorry I couldn't be there for you in your last moments. I know it's selfish of me, but I ask that you please stay by my side for all of mines now. Please be my guardian angel and watch over me," Pain said as he let the tears flow from his eyes. "I love you," he said as he released his emotions and cried over his brother's grave.

Pain knew it was time for him to let go of the thug mentality of chasing women and money. He was ready to step into his destiny and turn his life around.

No more would the dreams of change by drastic actions keep his head in the clouds. It was time to buckle down with the one thing that could help him get ahead in life: a plan and execution. He was determined to make things work for himself. He knew he had to start working on changing his dream. He thought back to a quote one of his mentors always favored: "Everybody has got to have a dream because, without them, what good is tomorrow?"

Pain knew his tomorrows were only going to get better and better as long as he stayed consistent and focused on being patient with his new job endeavor.

He took a look down at his brother's grave one more time before deciding to start his journey back home.